TO CLAIM A FAE

WINTER'S THORN, BOOK 3

MILA YOUNG

CONTENTS

To Seduce A Fae

To Tame A Fae

To Claim A Fae

The king is dead...

...and now my future, as my heart, hangs in the balance.

With the kingdom in chaos and my powers still fighting me for control, I'm left to wonder if there's even a place for me among the fae.

Or among the three men who have been there since the beginning of this journey.

Because even they feel like they're slipping away...

Especially since the court mage hates me and is conspiring against me at every turn.

But those aren't my only problems.

Finding the truth of who I am and what my destiny will be is consuming me and threatening to ruin all that I have and all those I love.

If I can't find a way to stop my enemies, we are all doomed and the fae realm will be lost.

And I can't let that happen. I won't. Even if it means a fight to the death...

Captivating conclusion to the 'WINTER'S THORN' saga.

FAE LEGENDS

The girl made of ash and shadows.

19 years ago

The world smells strange. Smoke. Rotting food. And sorrow. It leaks into the air like pollution. How can these humans live in such decay and filth? I scrunch up my nose.

These are my first steps on Earth, and I pray they'll be the last. Trees behind me sway from where I've emerged, and before me lays a flat road with lamps lighting the quiet area.

Soft gurgling sounds draw my attention to my baby in my arms, cradled against my breast. Her eyes are shut, and she sucks on her thumb, her nearly white hair laying across her forehead. So peaceful and perfect. My eyes prick, but I blink the tears away. The time for falling apart has long passed. This is for her. Everything is for her.

Hurriedly, I cross the road. The wind is vicious tonight, tugging at my cloak, ripping it off my head. I glance back into the silent woods, at the heavy moon that hangs low like a pregnant belly.

"Please Goddess, protect us," I whisper under my breath and rush forward. Old, worn buildings like square blocks line the sidewalk, and up ahead I see exactly what I'm after.

A bright yellow sign with the words *Women's Refuge.* The 'W' in the first letter flickers like it might snuff out.

My heart beats fast as my feet slap the ground.

Relle, my maid, found this place. She came to Earth and said no one would find it. When I glance around to the barren road, the decrepit homes, I have to agree. There is no way they'll find her here. No one will know.

She stirs in my arms, and my heart breaks when she looks up at me. Crystal blue eyes akin to mine. She smiles at me, and a tear escapes from the corner of my eye.

"Oh, little one." I choke on my words and press

her to my chest as I flee toward salvation. The lights are on inside, and I stand in front of the white building. Three steps lead up to the door, but I can't get my legs to move.

I stare down at my baby, and tears keep falling. She makes gurgling and cooing sounds, and they have me choking up. If only she knew the truth of why I can't keep her. Except, she can never find out or it'll kill her. Here, in this backward world, she stands a chance. In the Wandering Realm, her end is already planned.

"This is all I can give you." I move to sit on the steps and hold her on my lap. I draw out a small ribbon from my cloak pocket and wrap it around her tiny ankle. Her skin is so soft and warm against my fingers. I tie the knot loosely, leaving her embroidered name on the fabric. The least I can do is leave her with her nickname to make it a bit harder for her to ever find her way back home.

Guen.

Lifting her into my arms, I kiss her brow and inhale her beautiful powdery baby smell. I take in every bit about how she feels against me, the soft sounds she makes; everything I can, I memorize. It's all I'll have left of her.

I wipe my eyes, knowing I need to get going. The longer I'm gone, the more suspicion I'll raise.

On my feet, I turn toward the door just as it opens. Bright light beams from the hallway, and a middle-aged woman with the kindest eyes greets me.

"Hello, do you want to come in?"

I lick my dry lips, barely able to find my words. My chest is cracking in two, and it takes everything to not fall apart. I can't fall apart, at least not yet.

The woman motions with a hand for me to enter the house and steps aside in the doorway. Her aura swims in kindness. There's not a mean bone in her body, and I know now why Relle selected this house for my babe.

Up until now, I haven't cried, as I was too busy trying to not be caught, but now I can't seem to stop. My arms cling to Guendolyn like somehow I can keep her. The idea of staying here with her plays with me, teases me, but it's useless. My family will find me—they know my aura, and it'll lead them directly to me. But not my girl. I made sure no one would ever find her. As long as she stays here, the curse put on her should never come to pass. The glint of my magic, which will keep her concealed, still sparks in her. On Earth, she can just be a normal human and live a simple life rather than be hunted down.

"Is everything alright, ma'am?"

Startled by the woman's words, I lift my head and blink. I don't think as I hand my baby to her. "Please, will you hold her for a moment for me while I pull myself together?"

"Of course." She's a beautiful soul and scoops up Guendolyn, already cooing her a lullaby, rocking her in her arms.

My chin trembles, vision blurs with too many damn tears. Empty and barren is how I feel, my arms growing heavy from the loss.

When she's busy looking at the child, I slip away with the speed of the wind and pray I've done the right thing to keep Guendolyn safe.

When I'm across the road in the shadows of trees, I look back. I can't stop myself. The woman is in the doorway holding her, searching, calling for me. Then I turn and run.

I love you, my little fairy.

CHAPTER 1

GUENDOLYN

"The King of Shadow Court is dead! He's been murdered!" Ahren's advisor, Mael, declares from the doorway, his face pale and stricken with grief.

Silence falls over the bedroom. This has to be a mistake. So this... god no, please no, this has to be a mistake.

"What are you talking about?" Deimos asks, his voice still croaky from having just recovered from a Bloodcursed's bite.

Ahren suddenly bolts out of the room, Luther on his heels, their thumping footfalls fading somewhere in the corridors.

Just like that, in the span of a few seconds, our

world crumbles, and my stomach drops right through me.

The King of Shadow Court is dead.

My real father.

I finally found him, and he's been swept away. I can barely make sense of it.

Deimos stumbles from the bed, but the reality of what I heard from Mael collides into me. It crashes over me like powerful waves.

My whole life I've longed to know who my parents are, and when I find one, he's been murdered.

What the hell, universe? You hate me that much?

I had cured Deimos from the Bloodcursed's bite. Coupled with my memories from my past coming back to me, this should be a time to celebrate.

Instead, my knees wobble out from under me and they hit the floor, my stomach churning like I'm going to be sick. I can't even cry, because what stirs inside me isn't heavy grief but shock, sorrow and heartache of what's been ripped away from me. It's like I looked away for a few seconds and someone went into my room and stole everything I owned.

To have him ripped away breaks me. I spent one night with him, drinking and listening to his tales about fairies and fae, but it isn't enough.

Did he know who I was, or was he as oblivious as me?

Deimos is kneeling next to me, his arm around my lower back, drawing me toward him. I should be the one helping him, seeing as he was on death's door just a few minutes ago. Instead, I'm falling apart against his side and tucking my cheek to his chest. The moment he embraces me, the tears fall. He takes my hand and gives it a squeeze. His touch is overwhelmingly warm from being in bed so long, and he smells of perspiration, but I don't care.

Each breath comes hard. I never asked to be abandoned. Never asked to be born, either. And I hate those old feelings rising through me again. I worked for so many years with counsellors to learn to love myself and accept myself as I am, to convince myself that I'm not 'less than' because my parents left me alone in the world. Now, the familiar sensation of being abandoned forever claws through me, unravelling it all.

"It's going to be alright," Deimos whispers.

I look up at him, at this perfect man who

barged into my blissfully unaware life on Earth and brought me back here to remember how royally screwed my life is. But when I meet his gaze, my heart melts like ice under the summer's sun.

"What's going on? I didn't realize the king meant that much to you?" he asks softly.

"I don't know what to do. Tell me what I should be doing, Deimos." Confusion and agony rip through me again and again until I can't breathe.

He cups my face, his thumbs rubbing away my tears. "I don't understand, Guendolyn. What do you mean?"

I can't stop the growing ache in my chest, the one where I miss a man whom I barely knew and who I've searched for my whole life. But I shake my head. "Go see your father." I pull back, desperately wanting to drown in my loneliness, to let myself grieve and fall into the sorrow hacking at my chest. To be left alone as I come to terms with so much that I don't know where to start or end.

Deimos doesn't know that the king was my biological father. And this isn't the time to mention it, either.

He climbs to his feet and takes my hand gently. "Come with me to find out what happened."

I lower my gaze to my hands in my lap. "You go."

Silence.

I expect him to heave me to my feet and force me. Instead, the soft thump of his heels against the floorboard fades as he crosses the room. Seconds later, he's gone, and the door shuts behind him.

Everything happened too fast. I get up onto the couch and curl in on myself, hugging a pillow to my chest.

Snow drifts in slow motion outside the window against a backdrop of dark clouds. For years, I assumed when I found out who my parents are, I'd have closure. The likelihood of finding they had died was high, I'd told myself this. But at the end of the day, loss is loss, right? And still, it stings.

I don't remember how long I lay on the couch feeling sorry for myself, and when no one returns, I decide to head out and join the princes.

This isn't about me, now is it? It's about someone murdering the king. So, I open the door and find two guards swinging around to face me. Tall fae in dark uniforms who keep looking over their shoulders. They look just as worried as the rest about the king's death, and I don't blame them. I don't know enough about fae royal rules, but when a king falls, doesn't that make a kingdom vulnerable? I should have gone with Deimos in the first place.

"Can you take me to the princes, please?" I ask.

They nod, and we start walking fast along the dark hallway. It's like they'd been waiting for me to finally get my act together.

We cross the bridge between the princes' mansion and the royal castle. The breeze is icy against my skin. I hug myself, and quick steps bring me to the warmth of indoors. The mood in the castle hangs heavy, and guards run past us frantically. Other fae in silks and embroidered gowns and suits dart into rooms, their faces ashen. Their fear is palpable.

Moments later, I'm standing outside the doorway to the throne room. I hate this room. It brings back memories of me accidentally opening the portal to the Bloodcursed that hurt Deimos, and then another to the fairies. And now, the king has been killed here.

I don't move inside, a strange sensation crawling up my spine like I don't belong.

Luther consoles his crying mother, who buries her face against his chest. Ahren crouches near the body of the king, who's covered in a white bedsheet. Blood stains the material in large blotches, the red against the white a stark reminder of the loss. Deimos, still in his blue pajama pants and top, stands over the dead king, arms dangling by his side.

Mages are there too, including Jasion, along with a host of other men I don't recognize. Maybe close to thirty people are in the throne room, and no one pays me any attention. But all I can do is stare at the body.

He's the king.

My father.

I tell myself I have every right to be there and say my final words, but I can't get my legs to move.

So much blood.

Do I really want to remember him this way? I have so few memories of him, and the one night we did spend chatting, I cling to. That's the father I want in my thoughts.

I step back and bump into the guard who brought me here. "Please take me back." My voice trembles, but I don't care. This is too much.

"Follow me."

And I do just that. Hurried steps carry me away. I take one last look at the room and lock eyes with

Jasion, who stands in the doorway to the throne room.

Did he play a hand in the king's demise? The Ash King's mother asked me about him specifically. There are traitors in this castle, and for all I know, I could be the killer's next target.

His stare darkens, and a shiver runs down my spine.

Jasion must be involved... I know it in my bones, and I'll find a way to prove his guilt.

Deimos

"This is a shit show to wake up to." My attempt at lightening the mood in Ahren's study fails miserably. Neither he nor Luther respond. Ahren stares out the window, his back to me, while Luther sits in the middle of the room, his feet up on the table, crossed at the ankles and rocking back in his seat. He's miles away, staring into oblivion.

I'm in a strange state of both cheering that I survived the Bloodcursed's bite and my chest clenching with what we've lost. The king was the closest thing we had to a real father. Sure, he often kept his distance from us, but he tried, and it was more than we could ask for. Now, the grief pulsing through me is for a fae's life taken too soon and the agony my mother faces in losing her husband.

A knock comes at the door, and I turn. My brothers don't move, so I stroll over to find a maid in the doorway holding a silver platter with a jug and chalices. The sweet grape and cinnamon aroma finds me instantly. Spiced mead, only served when someone passes. My stomach growls at the smell, as it's been days since I've eaten.

"Enter," I instruct.

Not wasting a moment, she rushes in, places the offering on the table, and retreats.

Once she's gone, I serve myself a cup and take a drink, its warmth coating my insides as it slides down my throat. Still in my bedclothes and needing a bath desperately, I flop down into a seat at the head of the table and take my fill of the wine. I don't recall much from my time when I lingered on death's door, but I'm grateful the lethargy is gone. I doubt I'll be able to sleep for a week straight from the energy buzzing in my veins.

"Any thoughts on who killed him?" My voice slices through the silence.

"Many hate him," Luther muses. "Both in the court and outside."

"The killer was brazen. He got him in the heart, the blade driven down to the hilt. Whoever did this stood in front of him as he committed the murder," I state.

"There was no sign of a struggle," Luther adds. "Means it's someone he knew to get that close and for guards to see nothing."

"Unless they're in on the attack?" I suggest and glance over to Ahren. "What do you think?"

He doesn't look our way, just keeps staring out the window.

Luther cocks a brow. "What's the plan then?" he asks. "We all know what's coming next, right?"

Ahren turns his back to the snow-stained glass and leans against the frame, arms folded over his chest. He stares at me with contempt, but it's not aimed at me. He's the one that's going to save the day, and that means a massive sacrifice, whether he likes it or not.

"We delay the ceremony for as long as possible," Luther suggests.

Ahren growls under his breath. "How long?

Less than a week at most, then the vultures will pounce. The king's sister will race to our kingdom to claim the throne the moment she hears her brother has died."

I slouch in my seat and drink more of the warm wine, helping sate my empty stomach.

Luther drops his feet from the table and asks the question we've all been thinking. "You're the heir to the throne, Ahren, and to take ownership, you must be married. Who will you take as a bride?"

Guendolyn pops to mind. Mother will ask a million questions if we suggest her, as will the royal council. She'll need to know Guendolyn's family heritage, and Luther can't marry a non-royal. The big issue will be that Seelie and Unseelie are forbidden to wed, so that's not going to work.

Ahren knows this. The bitterness is scribbled over his tight expression. Each of us have fallen for Guendolyn, so how will she react to Ahren marrying someone else?

"I don't know the answer," Ahren answers truthfully. For once, he's not the older brother in control of every situation, but someone adrift in the chaos surrounding us. To lose someone and be forced to make such immediate decisions is fucked up. Letting another family member take the throne from Ahren will mean we lose our home and most likely will be kicked out of Shadow Court. So really, there is no other solution.

Ahren must marry a royal.

Footsteps echo outside the room, and the door suddenly swings opens.

We all glance at our mother as she steps inside. She pulls the black cloak tight around her neck, the embroidered golden swirls along the lapels glinting under the fireplace's blaze. It falls to her knees, and a blue dress dances around her ankles with each step she takes. Her crystal green eyes are red and puffy from crying, while bright white hair tumbles over her shoulders in curls. She holds herself tall and regal, even while her heart breaks. The lines around her mouth and eyes deepen, the signs of her aging more apparent today than previously.

I'm on my feet and reach her side, then take her into my arms. She softens against me and cries gently. Growing up, she'd always been a strong figure, someone who fixed our problems, who never gave up on us three. Now, she feels so small and weak in my embrace. I hold her tighter, needing to be there for her. We all do, just as she did for us when our father treated us like shit.

She breaks away from me and wipes her eyes. "These ridiculous tears refuse to stop. I left the mages and haven't been able to cease crying since."

Her crooked smile shatters me. She loved King Tibout dearly, and this kind of loss is gruesome.

"Come, sit down," I offer. Once she's comfortable, I pour her a serving of warmed wine. "You'll always have us."

She holds the goblet, running the tip of her finger over the rim, then lifts her head toward Ahren. He joins us at the table. The four of us sit around in silence. The last time we were in this state was when our mother announced she was leaving our real father and we had to leave our home that very night. It happened long ago, yet it feels like just yesterday when we were on the cusp of being homeless.

Ahren reaches across the table and places a hand on hers. "Everything will be alright. I will make sure of it."

She nods, but more tears thread down her cheeks. Luther's on his feet and retrieves a napkin from the cabinet behind him, then hands it to our mother. She wipes her eyes as he crouches behind her, hugging her, his chin propped on her shoulder.

"I've sent a message by crow," she finally tells us. "We can't waste a single moment." She sips the wine, all the while her eyes never leaving Ahren. Her hands shake.

He knows as well as we do that if Ahren doesn't marry, he'll lose the throne and we'll be out on our asses. Mother married into this family, so her taking the throne isn't an option.

"Who did you send it to?" he asks, stiffening in his seat.

"Our closest allies. Queen Titania."

I groan, as do Ahren and Luther on cue. She runs one of the two kingdoms in the east with her king.

"She's on her fourth husband," I quip.

"And the previous three all mysteriously vanished," Luther murmurs, glancing at our mother with raised brows.

"You believe those rumors?" She shakes her head. "I'm not marrying my son to the Queen, but her daughter. She is said to be a beauty unlike any other in the east. She will make a perfect partner and ensure your claim to the throne." Her words are directed at Ahren, even if he hasn't said a word.

"The Queen has been eager to merge our two kingdoms for a while now, which means the offer should be accepted before your stepfather's sister arrives to take the throne. I've postponed the funeral and forbid anyone from spreading the news about the king for a few days."

Ahren doesn't speak but pulls back his hand from Mother's while Luther moves back to his seat. Tightness gathers under Ahren's eyes. He holds himself composed, and I doubt anything could rattle his outside appearance. Different story on the inside.

This isn't an easy choice. Nope, not a choice at all, is it? He has no other option, and it kills me to watch him drown while there's nothing we can do. To save all of us, he has to carry the burden. And that's why he says nothing. Arguing won't change the situation we knew was coming, and any match he's paired with won't bring him closer to Guendolyn.

He wants her, like the rest of us, and his silence is the realization that he will lose her.

"You will be fine, Ahren, you'll see," Mother explains. "I barely knew King Tibout before I married into Shadow Court, and now I love him." She stands and pats down her cloak, her cheeks blushed, her eyes still spilling with tears. "Please keep this to yourself for now. Only a handful know. I will begin arrangements for the wedding in the meantime." She lowers her head and no one responds, plunging the room into a stifling silence.

His face reddens with fury, but if he says no, then we lose our home. And while he's alive, the second son can't take his place. I pity him, but I'll never show him that.

"We have a few days to the wedding," she states, her posture strong. Gone is our nurturing mother, replaced by a woman forced to take the lead to protect all of us. "We must be diligent and cautious until the killer is found in case they want you dead too, Ahren."

She turns on her heels and heads out of the room.

"Hell, Ahren," Luther blurts first. "What the fuck, man? Are you alright with this?"

Ahren's gaze narrows and he jolts to his feet, his chair scraping against the stone flooring. "What do you think?" he growls. "I'm fucking pissed, and I sure as hell don't want to marry someone else." His voice chokes. "But I don't have a choice, do I? I won't let our mother end up homeless." His pale green stare turns cold, his long white hair windblown, giving him a wild appearance. I swallow the boulder in my throat for him, as I can't begin to imagine how I'd feel if I were in his shoes.

"We knew this would come to pass one day. It's not a surprise," he says like he's trying to convince himself. Moments later, he says, "We don't tell Guendolyn, understand?"

"But—"

"No!" Ahren shuts down Luther. "Not yet, and I'll be the one to let her know when the time arrives." He marches out of the room, the door banging shut behind him. Luther clicks his tongue.

"This is cruel torture for him. You know he'll lose it and end up doing something stupid in his rage."

"Most definitely." I'm on my way to the door. "I'm going hunting or something. I need to get away from this shit."

I can't stand still, drowning in my thoughts. Ahren is fucked, and I don't know exactly how strong his bond is with Guendolyn, but from what I've seen, the news will break her.

CHAPTER 2

GUENDOLYN

I roll the red ruby over the back of my knuckles and flick it over my palm with a thumb, then repeat. Over and over. It's calming, in a strange way. The stone is cold against my touch, no matter how much I hold it. Then again, this isn't an ordinary rock, now is it?

It's the last crystal from the fairy queen's crown and belongs with the fairies, yet Hiss insisted it stay with me. Not to mention, it helps me open up portals with ease. Luther had said that the king had sold all of his mother's jewels in exchange for this stone from a witch fae who passed through Shadow Court. The king had been promised that the ruby would give him affinity with the fairies, which makes me wonder why he insisted on having it. Pure obsession, or something more?

Sitting cross-legged on the couch in Deimos' bedroom, I keep looking outside where the winds lash against the window and snow falls fast and heavy. The weather howls, and all I can picture are the tiny hive-style homes hanging from trees in the fairy village swinging wildly in the storm.

Since arriving in the Wandering Realm, if there's one thing I've learned, it's that nothing stays calm for long. Then there's the whole fairies helping me and calling me *Eirian*, a word for fairy queen, which confuses me even more.

I keep rolling the ruby over my knuckles, my thoughts wandering to Ash Court.

This is why Seelie and Unseelie can never be together. The Unseelie king's mother had said those words to me. She also added that the Unseelie bloodline comes directly from the fairy queen herself, which might explain my connection with them. And everything else she told me confirms the late king of Shadow Court had an affair with someone from the enemy kingdom. And yet, the king never knew he had a child. Why didn't my mother tell him?

The Unseelie king's mother had reveled in that

announcement. I hate her for that alone… and the fact she then tried to kill me, of course.

But I'm no fool. Whoever my mother is, she must be someone important. Why else would there be a war between the courts with me in the middle of it? I just hope she's still alive.

For so long, I was a pawn in their games.

The Unseelie king's mother had put the curse on me as a baby, and she gloated about it. I grit my teeth, as I barely escaped with my life... with the princes' lives. Something must be broken within me that the king's mother calls me an abomination. Or is that her demented view on anyone born to Seelie and Unseelie parents? The thought brings with it a reminder of the demented king's mother from Ash Court. Will she come after me again?

A groan from the doors sounds.

I quickly tuck the stone into the pocket of my pants and glance over my shoulder to Luther entering the room.

My heart pounds, while my stomach bursts with butterflies. I shouldn't be this excited about seeing a man I've been spending weeks with. Though, things aren't the same anymore. Not since I cured Deimos and Luther touched me while the magic still filled me. That touch had broken the spell that hid my memories from me. Now, my past with Luther is crystal clear in my mind, from his voice in my thoughts back on Earth, to the dirty things he'd say. There were the endless nights we spoke about stupid things, yet he captivated me all the same.

I know this fae inside and out, and the ache growing in my chest for him has everything to do with what he went through. He suffered on his own with our memories, and I couldn't do a thing to help him.

His keen gaze scans the room and rests on me. We're alone, and he kicks the door shut behind him. The gleam in his eyes calls to me. He looks at me differently, like we're long-lost lovers and we've finally found each other. The mischief in the quirk of his smile ignites the blaze in my chest. It's strange to think that I fell for his charm twice. Once before I even met him. And again while I couldn't remember much about our past.

We are meant to be together.

"I have a surprise for you." His deep baritone warms and comforts me.

I'm on my feet before I can make sense of how much influence he has over me.

"Luther." I rush to him and he collects me into his arms, lifting me off my feet.

Our mouths clash in an explosive match of emotions.

Arousal.

Desperation.

Unbearable need to make up for lost time.

His hands grab my ass, and his tongue slides into my mouth, dancing with mine. I lace my hands behind his neck and hold onto him, my legs wrapping around his hips. Our kiss is deep and passionate, the kind that knocks the breath out my lungs and leaves me dripping wet.

"You were saying?" I breathe the words.

One corner of his mouth curls upward into a lopsided grin with mischief gathering behind his gaze. Instead of answering, he kisses me and walks me back to the wall, where he pins me in place. The world fades around me; it's just us two at this moment.

No deaths.

No confusion.

No worry.

Only Luther and I.

Unable to resist or concentrate on anything, I

run my hands through his long, dark hair, drawing him closer. He's like a wind sweeping through my mind, awakening our past from the first time I laid eyes on him. Dark and menacing, and even then my knees wobbled in his presence with a desperation to connect. For so long we spoke in my thoughts, and I should have known then he'd always be in my life.

I grip onto him, gliding my tongue into his mouth, bucking my hips against his growing erection. Despite everything, if there's one good thing to come out of me discovering where I came from, it's finding three fae whom I adore and who want me just as much. I don't think I could bear to lose any of them.

They are my lifeline in this crazy realm. And I need more... so much more of each of them.

His lips drag over my cheek and to my neck, where he nibbles on the flesh before he pulls my earlobe into his mouth. Fingers slide under the fabric of my top, finding skin.

I arch and moan as his hand slides higher and cups a breast. I tip my head back against the wall and close my eyes as he grinds his cock against my heat.

This is where I long to be every day. I suck in

ragged breaths as he devours me, pinches my hardened nipple.

I cry out as he tugs on it, and my control is destroyed by his passion. Our lips once more merge. I kiss him with depth and passion, our tongues at war, then his teeth pull at my lower lip, the pain and pleasure a cocktail that leaves me dripping.

He draws back, our breaths racing, and slowly eases me back down on my feet, like that moment of fire was nothing more than a welcome kiss.

"What in the world was that?" I gasp, pulling down on my shirt to cover my stomach.

"You come running at me and I'm going to kiss you until you forget yourself." He slides a loose strand of hair behind my ear.

"That was so much more than a kiss, and you know it. You're an evil tease."

He lowers his hand from my hair, his knuckles gently brushing against my erect nipples. I gasp with a renewed flare of desire coiling tighter deep in my gut.

"Now *that* is a tease." He winks sexily at me. "What we did was different. I was preparing you."

I stiffen and narrow my gaze at him. "For what?"

"Told you I have something for you. And while I have every intention of fucking you, this isn't the right place... or maybe the time."

He cups my face and kisses me softly for a change. I consider protesting. Instead, I let myself fall for the distraction at a time when we need it most. His tongue licks over my lips, and I lean into his chest and whisper, "If you keep kissing me that way, I'm not responsible for what happens to your cock."

A burning gleam passes over his eyes, and the twitch of his erection pulses against my stomach.

"And you smell good enough to eat."

I draw in a shaky breath, waiting for my libido to stop sending waves of delicious arousal over me. "Damn, you're good."

He laughs, and I adore everything about him, but that sound he makes is extraordinary. "Remember who you're dealing with, little wolf. I'm the prince of darkness, a lord, a master." That grin brings back those exact words he'd said to me before we came to this realm.

"You're just as cocky as when you said that the first time." I lift my chin to him and smile back.

"It worked, didn't it? You melted over me. I remember when you first laid eyes on me; I saw the instant attraction you felt for me, the hunger in your eyes."

I half-laugh, refusing to let him know how right he is. "You're mistaking that for utter shock. I mean, at first, I almost mistook you for Dracula." I poke my tongue at him.

He grasps me by the arm and tugs me against him. "Who is Dracula?"

I burst out laughing. "It's a fictional character who's all dark and broody like you, but drinks people's blood to survive."

"Like the Bloodcursed?" He blinks as though trying to make sense of my ramblings.

"Yes and no. Anyway, I remember you once saying to me that long ago, darkness and light came together and created beauty… a beauty that will destroy this world. You were talking about me. Why didn't you tell me back then I was a fae?"

"Would you have believed me?"

I shrug and want badly to say yes, but it'd be a big fat lie. "So, where's this surprise you promised me?"

His hand slides into mine and our fingers inter-lace. He guides me toward the door and out into the hallway. "Patience," he says.

"Will you stay with me today?" I ask as we

stride down the corridor where a maid shuffles past us, her head low.

"I'm not going anywhere. Now or ever. Just remember that, little wolf. No matter what happens, you will always have me by your side."

I glance over at him—his words are peculiar, but I think nothing of it once we pause in front of a black arched door.

"Hmm, should I be scared?" I ask.

"You tell me." He pushes the door and it swings open.

Before us lies a round room with white stone walls and floor, along with long narrow windows akin to the ones in the bedrooms. In the middle of the room sits a round pearl-white tub, big enough for five or six people to sit inside. It sits flush on the floor with no feet, and it must weigh a tonne. A small set of wooden steps rests on one end of the bath, and the other has a table with an array of fruit and breads and cheeses.

Steaming heat curls up from the water, waiting for us. "This is so perfect. But seriously, what is it with fae and baths?"

"It's a luxury not many have, and we use it to relax. Now, are you stripping, or am I doing it for you?" He releases my hand and starts grabbing at my top.

I slap his hand and push him away. "Are Ahren and Deimos joining us too?" With the tragic news, I want us all together.

"Deimos has gone hunting, and Ahren needs time alone right now. So you're stuck with me."

I guess everyone deals with death differently, and I welcome a bit of luxury, so I fumble with the buttons on my pants and take off my shoes.

When Luther doesn't move, but stares at me, gaping like he might drool, I say, "You just going to watch?"

"Is that a problem?" He strides toward me, and I back away, recognizing the look on his face. My insides burn up from his intense stare.

"I can get undressed on my own."

"Then hurry." His voice grows deep, like his control is on the verge of vanishing.

I force myself to turn away from him to not give him the satisfaction of seeing everything. Then I muse, "Any chance you could arrange for a drink? Something warm?"

Over my shoulder, I find him looking at the platter of food that lacks drinks.

He narrows his gaze at me and huffs. "I'll be right back."

The moment he shuts the door behind him, I sprint to the bath while ripping my clothes off in record time, leaving a trail in my wake. Up on the steps, I step onto the seating platform that runs along the inside wall of the tub. The water is scorching hot, but at the same time it feels incredible to sink into its embrace. The water is like silk, gliding over my body. I slip my head under its surface and stay submerged for as long as I can hold my breath.

It's a strange thing to crave numbness. I keep telling myself the king might have been my father, but only by blood, yet I also think I should grieve more than I am.

I push my head up and out of the water, my eyes flipping open only to come face to face with Luther staring down at me.

He drags his top up and over his head before tossing it behind him. Then he's pulling at the buckle on his pants as his gaze travels over my body in the water. It's nothing he hasn't seen before, but it doesn't ease the blush spreading over my cheeks. Seconds later, he's naked and climbing in. I tell myself to look away but fail miserably—I can't help but take in his cock, large and partially hard. I recall how big he gets once he's at full mast, how incredible it feels inside me. A shiver curls over my clit just at the thought.

I splash around as I attempt to maneuver as far from him as possible to give him space, only managing to slide on the smooth surface of the tub and dip underwater.

Frantically flaying about to get my balance like the most uncoordinated goldfish in the world, I grab for the edge of the tub. Strong hands snatch my ankle and haul me across the tub, dunking me further.

Holding my breath, I struggle and finally burst out of the water, gasping for air.

Luther's sitting on the ledge in the bath, legs spread and me between his thighs, laughing at me.

I wipe my eyes and push my hair out of the way, then splash him in the face. "If you're trying to drown me, you're doing a fine job."

"I thought you could swim?" He mocks me with his words and mirth.

With a roll of my eyes at him, I spin away from him. Strong hands grasp my hips, and he drags me backward until I'm sitting right on his lap. My bare ass on his thigh, his cock nestled against the side of my leg as I am turned to my side.

"I want you close to me." An arm locks around my stomach, and he's pretty much eye level with me. "You don't need to be shy around me, little wolf. I adore every inch of you, and if I could have my way, I'd spend every second in your company. And you would be naked, of course."

"Really? And you?"

"I'd be at your mercy." He blows me a kiss.

"You're such a sweet talker."

He shuffles us around so we are sitting on the ledge sideways, and I slip down to sit right between his legs. My back presses against his hard chest, his cock cradles my back, and his arm coils around me like he has no intention of letting me go. He brushes my hair over one shoulder, then kisses the back of my neck and shoulders. My skin pricks with goosebumps from the excitement building within me. But he never does anything more.

At first, I'm confused. I had this impression he carried every intention to finish what we started in the bedroom. Except, he holds me tight like he just needs the company.

A knock raps at the door, and I straighten.

Luther draws me back as the door opens. His arms lower to cover my breasts, which I appreciate. My knees are bent in front of me up on the ledge.

Dana waltzes in, the older maid who remembers me from last time. "Excuse me, Your Highness." She comes in with another maid, both of them carrying bundles of towels and clothes and shoes. They place the items at one end of the room on a side table, then they retreat and shut the door.

"Thanks for covering me up." I glance over my shoulder at this smoldering hot fae, whose dark hair is wet and pushed off his face. Thick brows crown the most spectacular amber eyes. My gaze drops to his full lips, tempted to lean in and taste them again.

"You got it wrong," he murmurs. "I wasn't concealing you, little wolf, but making it very clear that I've claimed you as mine by holding onto your gorgeous breasts in front of them."

My breath catches as I remember he's mine now too, and I can't help but love how protective and proud he is of me. I almost lost him because I couldn't remember our time together. Now, I want to soak him up and not lose another moment.

"The more I learn about your ways, the more you remind me of a hierarchy of wolves." I soften into his arms, the hot water brushing against my shoulders.

He kisses my head. "That's probably the most accurate way I've heard it described. And there are many factions vying for power." He traces his fingers across my palms, sending shivers through me. "When I find the person responsible for today's atrocity, they won't die a quick death."

I hold onto Luther's arm around me, my mind racing in dozens of directions when a thought slips past my lips. "Why would someone kill the king?"

"Usually power," he answers. "Or revenge, but I'm suspecting it's about power to weaken our court more than it already is."

"Between us," I begin, "I wonder if Jasion might be capable of such a gruesome act." The moment the words leave my mouth, I regret them. I'm pointing fingers to the mage based on my instinct, on my dislike for him, but does that make him a murderer? Maybe... hell, I don't know.

"Jasion has been part of our inner court since a young age, as were his father and father before him." Luther frowns. "But I don't trust him. Haven't liked him since we first met so long ago. He'd always make snarky remarks at Deimos and me when Ahren wasn't around as we grew up. But I'm not sure he is a killer type."

"No, forget I said anything." Maybe the Unseelie king's mother was trying to get under my skin. Make me see guilt where there was none, to cause derision. And just because I don't like the guy doesn't mean that he's a murderer.

"What would he have to gain?" Luther continues.

I shrug because I don't know the answer. "Anyway, let's not talk about that. I'm starving."

He reaches over to the table and collects a bunch of black grapes. He plucks one and places it into my mouth, the fruit exploding with sweetness over my tongue.

Not for a moment do I mind. If this Adonis wants to feed me and treat me like a princess, then I say *more please*. Maybe for a change, things might finally calm down so I can wrap my head around where exactly I fit in the Wandering Realm.

Candles flicker wildly across the dining table, and darkness cloaks the rest of the room. I'm sitting next to Deimos, with Luther directly across from me and Ahren on my right. Since arriving back at Shadow Court, I've longed for us all to be together, but there's a strange feeling in the air tonight. A sense of tension which I put down to the shitty day. Still, it nags me, as I hoped being with the three princes would help us all. But it isn't.

I reach over and fill my plate with a slice of roasted rabbit and vegetables. My mouth waters, and I scoop a bite into my mouth. Maple glazed, I moan at the crunch of the potatoes and how fluffy they are on the inside. Quickly, I collect four more with the serving spoon.

The princes don't seem to notice. Deimos eats directly from the platters, unable to put enough into his mouth. He has a fresh cut across his cheek, blushing pink, but I don't ask him what happened. Luther had told me he went out hunting, and if that's his escape, I respect his decision.

Luther only eats meat, nothing else, and when I watch him cutting slices and eating them hungrily, all I can remember is the two of us in the tub earlier today, talking, laughing, embracing. He fills out his deep mocha-colored coat so well, leather buckles taut across the front instead of buttons. There's no mistaking the attraction I hold for him. His black hair is draped off his shoulders, a thin layer of growth on his jawline, and my body awakens at the memory of him naked against me. My stomach flip-flops at how much I crave him… crave all three princes.

Ahren isn't eating but staring into the darkened corners of the room.

I lower my fork to the table. "Ahren, are you alright?"

He doesn't respond but remains distant. The other two glance up, looking over to their brother.

"Ahren, you with us?" Luther asks with a calm voice.

The eldest prince blinks and turns his attention to the three of us. "What did I miss?" He helps himself from the ceramic bowl of stew and begins eating as if none of us are watching him.

Luther looks my way. The corner of his mouth quirks, coaxing my own smile. His feet under the table clasp around mine. Every inch of me responds to him, screams for more.

Deimos tilts his head in my direction, his hand sliding onto my thigh, fingers pulling the fabric of my skirt up my legs.

I tense and push his hand away, tucking my legs back from Luther's reach. I'm not a prude, but right now, I am more concerned for Ahren and need to know he's okay.

"Ahren, do you have plans tomorrow?" I ask just as the door to the great hall opens. Footfalls echo around us as several maids hurry inside with platters of cakes and fruit and cheese.

"I'm busy," Ahren replies, not even looking at me.

I swallow hard and try not to overthink his reaction. Everyone is quiet tonight, and it's understandable, so I let it go. Sorrow is a close friend of mine. I focus on my meal while the maids squeeze the desserts onto the table. I've always been a sucker for sweets, and the three-tiered chocolate cake has my name written all over it.

"Would you like a piece?" Deimos asks, having seen me drool over the treat. "It's the sweetest plum cake."

"Plum? Not chocolate?"

Luther leans back in his seat, grinning like the Cheshire cat, which feels appropriate for the realm I've fallen into here. "There's no such thing as chocolate here, little wolf."

I frown. "The cake looks like it could be."

Deimos places a wedge on a clean plate, and I have my fork ready when he hands it to me. Even before it touches my tongue, I smell the fruit, but I don't care and stuff it into my mouth, wanting it desperately to be chocolate.

Sweetness spreads over my mouth—super sweet—the icing buttery and more like blueberry jam than chocolate. I won't lie, disappointment sweeps over me, but beggars can't be choosers, right? I finish the slice.

Ahren's on his feet. "I'm calling it a night." Without another word or even a glance my way, he turns and strides toward the door.

Nothing feels right about his behavior. I get he is grieving, but so are his brothers, and they can look me in the eyes and talk to me. They are super affectionate—in fact, more than before—so what's up Ahren's ass?

I stew over his behavior. When the door shuts behind him, I push away from the table. My chair scrapes on the stone floor and I scramble to my feet.

"Guendolyn?" Deimos asks.

"I'll be back. I just need to do something. Don't eat all the cake," I tease as Luther reaches for a slice.

Out in the hallway, Ahren strides down the corridor quickly, his shoulders curving forward like he carries the world's problems on them. We've been through too much together, he's shared personal things about himself with me, and I want to be there for him. Whether he wants it or not.

Guards are stationed along the marble hallway and down every passage I travel. With Ahren moving faster now, I quicken my pace.

He suddenly glances over his shoulder at me, shadows dancing his darkening eyes. "You have no subtlety when you track someone."

"Yeah, well, I wasn't trying to sneak up on you."

I close the distance between us as he slows down but never stops completely.

I look up at him and wait for him to say something, but he never does. I reach for his hand, my fingers finding his warm skin. He doesn't flinch, but he doesn't hold my hand either. Worry coils at the base of my gut, and with it comes a fear that he doesn't want to be with me. A lot of things scare me, and I've conquered many of those fears, except when it comes to the princes, my bravery dissolves.

For now, I tell myself it's him grieving.

"Was thinking we can spend time together to talk," I offer.

It's only when we reach the door that leads to the bridge between the castle and mansion that he pauses. Two guards flank the door, and I feel uncomfortable having them listen to us.

"It's best you return to my brothers for dinner. With the king's passing, I won't have time for you." His voice is flat and cold. Icy shards spear through my chest as he stares right through me.

This isn't Ahren. "What's going on?" I hate that my words come out as a whisper, that the guards are witness to my despair.

The prince turns away from me and shoves

open the door before stepping into the windy night across the bridge.

I shudder at the way he dismisses me. Heavy layers of dread drag through me that something else is wrong here. I look over to the guards, who glance away at my stare.

I don't even wait for the door to shut before I rush out after Ahren, fury burning me that he'd treat me this way.

"Hey!" I call out.

He pauses on the bridge, keeping his back to me.

Night drapes the kingdom around us, the sky bright with stars where the clouds have parted.

Hair blows in my face, and I push it behind my ears. My skin ripples from the freezing wind buffeting into me.

"You want to tell me what's going on?" My steps toward him are awkward as I hug myself. The skirt whips around my legs, and despite the cold, my insides are on fire with emotions.

"There's nothing to tell, Guendolyn. Don't make this harder than it is."

The words slice into me like blades. "What are you talking about?" I grab his arm, but he pulls away. My heart splinters, the ache in my chest deepening. "You don't have to go through the loss of your stepfather alone. Please Ahren. Let me in."

He keeps his head low, his breaths deep and ragged. The dull ache rising through me deepens, and I know in that moment without a shadow of a doubt that his reaction has little to do with the king's demise. It's about us. I feel it in my body.

"Did I do something wrong?" I whisper, hating that I sound so hopeless. Except this isn't anguish, but the tearing of the bond I thought we shared. In those few moments when he doesn't respond, a storm of feelings sweeps over me.

Sorrow that I'll lose him.

Pity for myself.

Fury at him for pulling this shit.

And most of all how I want to force him to look me in the eyes and tell me the damn truth of what's going on.

"Over the coming weeks, there will be changes in the court. I'll take the throne, and..." His voice fades, and at first I don't think he's going to respond. Then he says softly, "I can't do this, Guendolyn."

I tremble, fighting the panic clawing at my chest. I lash out and snatch his arm, forcing him to face me. "So you won't have time for me? Is that what you're worried about?"

"I'd rather you hate me. That I can deal with, but your tears will destroy me."

I stare at him, bewildered. I want time to stand still, to pause everything and let myself catch up on what's happening. But my mind is melting, and the words slip past my lips like unstoppable lava from an erupting volcano.

"Are you breaking up with me?"

Does he even understand that concept? I don't know, don't care as everything inside me starts to fall apart.

"I have a responsibility," he says, like I'm his guard or one of his servants.

"Fuck responsibility," I snap. "I thought we had..." My eyes prick with the tears pooling and rolling down my cheeks. "What's happening, Ahren?"

He doesn't move to take me into his arms as I expect him to. It's only us two, the wild weather roaring around us, and the crack of my heart.

"Look around to where you are," he starts with a frustrated tone. "I'll be in every council meeting, visiting other courts, dealing with Ash Court, the Bloodcursed, never being home. I'll have to make hard decisions that I already hate myself for, that you will hate me for. Fuck, this isn't what I want, and I wish I could tell you we'll make this work, but I won't break your heart by keeping you in the shadows. You deserve so much more."

The anger fades from his face, his eyes shining in the moonlight. This gorgeous fae captured my attention from the first time we met. He shared with me his past struggles, his agony, his dreams, but maybe I was a fool to believe anything could happen between us. I had known he was destined for the throne as the heir, but everything happened too fast to truly acknowledge what that meant.

He's already made up his mind.

Clouds slide over the moon, stealing the light and darkening his expression. He looks angrier now. My stomach clenches as he draws in sharp breaths.

"You are wrong," I whisper. "Because you've already broken me."

"Oh, Guendolyn." His voice shakes. But a split second is all it takes for the stoic prince to return in front of me. He straightens his posture, standing stiff against the strong wind tugging on his coat and long white hair. It flutters in the air like a flag.

"You'll understand soon enough. And then you'll hate me."

My chest clenches at his words. As much as it kills me, I do nothing as he turns and marches away. Desperation blooms through me once more, stronger this time. I curl my hands into fists, refusing to be the one who runs after him. I may not make sense of his reasoning, but he's made his choice, hasn't he?

My first instinct is to leave this realm, but I've given my heart to three fae. And I refuse to lose Luther and Deimos because Ahren is being an asshole. They mean the world to me. And today… well, today is just too much for me.

I've lost my father and one of my men.

I rush across the bridge and make a line for my bedroom, tears blurring my vision, my throat tightening to the point where I can barely breathe.

CHAPTER 4

AHREN

I lean against the wall outside Guendolyn's room. No idea what time of the night it is, but there's not a soul in sight. It's too late, but I can't sleep or silence my mind. Add to that my gut aches and twists in on itself, and I feel like utter shit. I'd been unprepared for this catastrophe, and now I'm drowning.

This wasn't how anything was meant to go. In truth, I still hadn't worked out how to keep Guendolyn with us for a future together, but letting her go had never crossed my thoughts.

Now I can't get her sweet voice, the tears in her eyes, the devastation on her expression out of my head. It strangles me, and I came here to try to do something. To make it right somehow.

A guttural moan rips from my throat, hands curling into fists. My emotions whip back and forth between the grief of letting her go and fondness at memories I will cherish forever. Those lips so sweet, so soft, so captivating, just like her.

I should be paying this much attention to uncovering the king's killer and making them suffer. I'm fucking furious for having the one thing I desperately want taken away. My priorities have changed now to Guendolyn.

I turn to the door, staring at the handle, and I play with the idea of going inside, breaking down the door if I have to for one last kiss, one more everything. Who the fuck am I fooling? There is no 'one last' anything, is there? It will never be enough.

Pitching one hand to the wall, I can't see straight through the fury burning within me. Revenge bubbles in my chest. When I find the sonofabitch, I'll rip them apart with my bare hands for putting me in this spot.

Except, what I want doesn't matter anymore. Not if I want to keep a roof over my family's heads. It's what mother wants, what the king had insisted on. And something I've dreamed of since we moved here. I was so young then, and I trained endlessly for this position, aspired to take my place on the throne. Now, I'm torn.

I never expected Guendolyn to sweep into my life and steal my heart.

Fuck!

I suck in one raspy breath after another, nails digging into my palms as I squeeze my fists. Wrenching my gaze from her door, I turn away.

This is for the best.

I goddamn hate those words. Nothing is better for me than Guendolyn, and it cuts me deep to make this decision. When the hell had she crept into my heart so much, anyway?

I blink and wait for my reasoning to catch up to the heartache of hurting her. I'll accept my pain, but it's unbearable to watch her cry.

One last look toward Guendolyn's room and I stride away. My presence won't help. It'll make it harder for both of us, and I won't entertain that idea. I'll keep my distance, as much as it kills me. I'll follow the rules and do the right thing for everyone else.

I'll sacrifice my heart.

Guen

*B*ruised clouds shift over the sky, stealing the morning sun outside, the view spectacular through the floor-to-ceiling windows in the dining room. I stir honey into my porridge and take another mouthful. The room is empty. No signs of the princes this morning.

Rage roared inside my head and chest at Ahren for most of the night, and when I finally slept, my dreams were filled with me running from darkness. Out of that darkness, a voice came, calling for me. It reminds me of the dreams and visions I experienced growing up. The twisted woods and lurking danger. The images I painted of them, having no clue how much of a significance they had to me. Guess the truth has been dying to come out all along.

Now I sit here drifting away in sorrow, my mind heavy with questions I have no answers for. But I force myself to finish my food and wash it down with juice.

I refuse to accept Ahren's decision to push me away, and his brothers are bound to know what's really going on with him. But I also need a distraction before I wear a hole in my bedroom from pacing.

Outside the dining hall, my guard waits for me. "Michae, can we visit the throne room, please?"

He nods without pause, and we stride down the corridor. Michae is a tall fae with short blond hair and pointy ears. Like most of the soldiers, he's broad and intimidating. Luther appointed him as my personal watchdog, and if anyone questions who I am, I'm to continue the ruse that I'm the princes' personal healer.

Like the previous day, there are fae darting about the castle in a frenzy.

I wrench my gaze toward the throne room as we approach. The door is shut. Michae pushes it open, and I step into the empty hall made of marble. The place is spotless, without a hint of blood or the chaos that took place here. It's a grand, large space with columns creating a passage down the middle leading to a wide staircase.

"Have they found anything on the murder?" I tilt my head back to look at Michae.

His attention sweeps to the top of the marble steps to an empty black throne. "Still can't believe our king is gone."

It's where Ahren will sit as he rules the Shadow

Court, and with that thought comes the ache in my chest. He pushed me away. Insisted it's due to responsibility, but I listened to the cracks in his voice. This isn't what he wants, so I need to dig and find out the truth, to make him understand there is always a way to make us work.

I refuse to walk away. We were just beginning to bond, to get closer, and I will break down the gates of hell itself if it means I can claim him back.

"Not much," Michae says, pulling me out of my thoughts. It takes me several moments to remember what I had asked him. "But you know what's strange?" He leans in close to me. "Apparently there were traces of clove powder near his body. Either the fae who did this is clumsy or it was a deterrent."

"Clove, the spice? That's unusual."

"The kitchens and staff working there are being investigated by the mages."

The clue leaves me confused, but a clue is a clue, so maybe they'll find the person responsible soon enough. The idea of a killer roaming the castle who may have his eye on Ahren next makes me sick to my stomach.

Michae walks deeper into the throne room and pauses at the base of the steps, lost in thought.

My hands are in the pockets of my riding pants, since it was all the maids had available and I was tired of how inconvenient dresses were. Clasping the cold ruby calms me. It has this way of bringing all my focus to the middle of my core rather than to hundreds of other distractions.

Sniffles sound, and I tilt my head sideways to gain a better view of Michae. I am convinced he is crying for the loss of his king.

I step closer to the spot where I remember seeing the late king on the ground, rolling the ruby over my knuckles. To lose my father sits heavy on my chest. I grieve the notion of losing him, not necessarily the man himself, who I didn't know well enough. Which makes me want to find my mother so much more. To uncover what happened between her and my father, why they gave me away, and so many other whys that the muscles in my shoulders bunch up.

Don't get your hopes up, I keep telling myself.

"Are you permitted to be in here?" a male's voice barks.

I flinch at his abruptness, the ruby almost bouncing out of my hand, but I snatch it out of the air and stuff it into my pocket.

Behind me stands Jasion, and a shiver crawls

down my spine. He's wearing his mage clothes—a black robe-skirt that falls to his ankles, metal chains around his waist, and a fairy skull that is fist-sized hangs from his bare neck. After meeting Hiss and having the fairies save me several times now, I sneer at the way he carries that skull like a trophy. I want to rip it off him. I hated this mage from the first time I met him, and my distaste for him hasn't changed.

Michae steps alongside me. "We were just leaving," he announces and takes my elbow to rush me out of the room.

I hold Jasion's gaze as we pass him, and if someone could spew hatred from their stare alone, this mage would be loathing me to the moon and back. It has to do with Ahren, this I know. Luther mentioned in the carriage on our way to Ash Court that Jasion might have a crush on Ahren, which would explain his evil eye at me.

With hurried steps, we make quick work on vanishing down a corridor that takes us straight to the bridge outside.

I glance over my shoulder, almost feeling Jasion's eyes still on me.

Michae murmurs, "He sneaks around the castle, but no one knows what he does." My guard finally lets go of my elbow, and we walk at a normal pace through the hall.

"Hasn't he been working at the castle for most of his life?" I ask, recalling the bits of information I learned from the princes.

Michae cuts me a sarcastic look. I'm starting to really like this guy. He leans closer, whispering, "The maids tell me they find all kinds of dead animals and birds in his room, that he tortures them."

I gasp. "Have they told Ahren?"

Michae stares at me as if I've grown horns. "Unless the maids want to suddenly disappear, they keep quiet. Jasion is a very vengeful mage."

The truth of his words doesn't surprise me, but it worries me. "Did the king and Jasion get along?"

Michae raises a brow. "The king didn't like his wildness and disobedience, but he appreciated that Jasion carried strong powers, more so than the other mages. It's that old saying, *sup with the devil.*"

I nod as the shivers return to my skin and remind me to keep my distance from the mage even more.

When I reach my room, I head inside and kick off my shoes while Michae stands guard outside.

A hard knock raps on the door, and I snap

around, expecting my guard to tell me I forgot something.

Instead, it's Jasion standing in my doorway, glowering.

Oh, hell. What does he want?

CHAPTER 5

GUENDOLYN

"My apologies for not coming to you earlier," Jasion says. "May I come inside?"

Michae stands behind him in the hallway to my room, waiting for me to respond so he can have any excuse to get rid of Jasion. Except, is it a good idea to anger a mage who tortures animals in his chamber? *Keep your enemies closer,* floats in my mind.

I nod. "Michae, please join us too." Which he eagerly does, leaving the door open.

Jasion cuts the guard a hard side look. "These are not matters to be discussed in front of you. Wait outside," he commands.

I stiffen. "Michae, you are fine to stay," I reconfirm.

Jasion's lips thin, but I don't care. This is my room, and I honestly don't want to be alone with him. Every time I've spent time with him in the past, I ended up feeling like a bug under a microscope.

He steps into my room, chest sticking out, distaste twisting his lips.

I retreat and lean up against the back of the couch, hands on either side of me, gripping the wooden frame. Where I am as far from him as possible without it looking obvious.

"What did you want to see me about?" I ask, grasping onto every thread of confidence I have.

"I like to get to know anyone who works closely with Ahren. As you can appreciate, since he is going to be the king soon."

I lick my dry lips, trying to make sense of what exactly he wants. "You are worried about him?" I ask.

He bows his agreement with a small tilt of his head, the fairy skull around his neck swinging slightly. "I knew you were smart."

I bristle at his patronizing tone. Stupid asshole.

But I smile because I'd rather he think I'm some dumb female healer.

He rubs a hand over his mouth as he strolls toward the window. "I've been told you are getting close to Prince Luther as well. The walls in this kingdom have eyes."

Michae stands tall near the door, shrugging when I glance his way. I turn to Jasion, who remains with his back to me. The wind howls bitterly outside. The storm may have passed, but even with the fireplaces, these large rooms and halls never fully warm up. What I wouldn't give for my electric blanket and an outlet about now.

"I'm not following your point?" I play the person he expects of me.

"Of course not." He pivots toward us, the material of his long mage-skirt flaring around his ankles. "Many who come to the kingdom to work for the princes dream up ideas of how to stay here longer." He closes the distance between us. "You're a pretty girl who I'm sure spreads her legs easily, but—"

"Don't speak to me that way," I snap, squaring my shoulders, facing this mage. I don't give a shit who he is, I have powers too, used them with the king's mother in Ash Court, and I won't bow down to this prick.

He raises a brow and doesn't show a hint of being taken aback by my retort. He's good, I know that, and he's rattled me, but I won't show it. No matter how much my heart hammers in my chest, how much my knees shake.

"Remember your place," he says calmly, like I have no control of myself.

Fire lashes over my chest that he says that to me. Fucking asshole.

"I witnessed the tension between you and Ahren last night, and I'm here out of the goodness of my heart to help you."

The moment between Ahren and I on the bridge flashes in my mind, the time when he tore my heart to shreds. Jasion had been watching us? The prick!

I scoff a bit too loudly, which has him straightening his spine.

His eyes narrow at me. "I realize I'm wasting my time, so I'll make this short." He steps closer to me, as does Michae from his spot by the door.

A shiver worms its way down my spine, but I won't retreat, no matter how desperately I want to. I loathe how close Jasion stands in front of me. It's intended to intimidate, and for that reason, I dig in my heels and raise my chin to face him straight on.

"Ahren and the princes are royal. They have slept with many commoners like you in the past, but that is all you are to them, little girl. Ahren needs someone stronger by his side. Someone with the ability to guide him, someone with a royal bloodline. You are not worthy, and I recommend you pack your bags and leave before it's too late."

My blood boils, rage pulsing in my ears. I want to wipe the smug grin off his face. "You're a petty asshole, but let me give you a piece of advice while we're sharing. Ahren loves women way too much, so if you think you have a chance in his bed, then don't waste your time. He'll reject your ass so quick, you won't know what hit you."

I suck in each sharp breath, my pulse raging in my veins. This isn't like me, but right now he has me so angry, a faint thread of power sweeps over my chest and down my arms like it did back at Ash Court. What would he do if I tossed him through a window?

My lips quirk into a grin.

His face flushes red, shoulders rising.

Oh, shit, I definitely hit a soft spot.

The air thickens in the room. Michae clears his

throat uncomfortably, while I wonder if I can even draw on whatever power I have before this mage attacks.

Jasion's hand lashes out and snatches me by the throat. He's so fast, I barely have time to raise my hands to stop him. Iron fingers squeeze, and the pain is excruciating, like he might tear my head right off. Panic slams into me as I glare into his darkening pupils. Michae rushes to us.

Jasion hurls his hand in the guard's direction, and a spray of powder splashes Michae. He flies backward, colliding into the wall.

I dig at Jasion's fingers around my throat, my lungs burning for oxygen. This isn't how I was meant to die, and with fear curling around me, I can't even focus on my power.

I strike my hand at his face and claw my fingernails down his cheek, breaking the skin.

He growls and throws me aside with such strength, my legs crumble under me and I smack the ground with my hip hard.

Scrambling backward, I don't feel the ache; only how fast my heart beats, how I was stupid to think I stood any chance against this monster. I'm gasping for each breath, my gaze never leaving him.

He turns to me with fury burning in his eyes. Blood drips down his cheeks from the two scratches I gave him. The bastard deserves so much worse.

Nostrils flaring, he comes for me, fist raised. His face darkens, and he resembles a demon in that moment, ready to strike me repeatedly until I can't take another breath.

I frantically dig my hand into my pocket for the ruby, my only thought to escape, to get out, or even call the fairies. I don't know exactly how to do that, but it doesn't stop me from trying. Power erupts deep in my chest.

But he moves too fast, and panic takes me.

I cover my head, cowering, the stone clasped in my fist.

Someone darts into the room in a sudden flash.

Deimos.

Oh my god, thank you.

He snarls and leaps onto Jasion's back, locking an arm around his throat and wrenching him backward.

Jasion jerks his head back, his hand diving into one of the small leather bags hanging from his belt. But when he glances up to see it's Deimos, his face turns snow white.

His body slackens, and he slips his hand free from the pouch.

"Your Highness," he gurgles.

"You like to hurt women?" Deimos snarls like a lion. He releases the mage and spins him around by the shoulder.

Then his fist flies at Jasion's face. Over and over. He knocks him off his feet. Deimos is wild and never stops. He drops to one knee and pounds like a machine.

Blood and groans.

I don't look away, not for a second. I'd like to say it's too gruesome and violent, but Jasion deserves that and so much worse. My chest blooms at seeing my prince fight for me. There's no hesitation, and I adore him in that moment more than I thought possible.

Michae stumbles toward them, shaking his head as if his vision is blurry.

The mage cries out, his hands pushing against the prince, but he never strikes back, never uses magic. Guess he knows that's instant death.

Michae firmly sets a hand on the prince's shoulder.

Deimos finally stops his assault, his fist bloody. Jasion draws in raspy breaths, his eyes puffy, lips torn open. There's so much blood. I should feel pity, but I am cheering on the inside.

Deimos gets to his feet and looks over to Jasion. "Get the fuck out of my face before I rip your spine out. You touch her again, and I'll keep my word." He swings his attention over to a bewildered Michae. "Get him out of here, now!" Then my prince takes long strides toward me, his eyes flooded with worry.

He cups my face with a clean hand, studying me. "Did he hurt you? I'm going to murder him if he did."

I shake my head but his gaze falls to my neck where it burns from Jasion's fingers. "I'm fine. You arrived before he could do worse."

He draws me into his arms, holding me so tight I can't inhale, but I don't want to push him away. Not when I'm shaking all over from the attack.

Deimos breaks from me and watches as Michae drags the mage out of the room. "Why did he attack you?"

"He came here to tell me I wasn't worthy of royalty. He pissed me off, so I provoked him by saying Ahren is into girls and he doesn't stand a chance."

Deimos bursts out laughing. "That's my girl.

There's no doubt now Jasion is so head over heels infatuated with my brother that he'd do anything to get rid of the competition. So, he's staying locked up until all this shit is over."

I blink at him. "The funeral?" My mind echoes with Jasion's words about not being worthy, about royal blood. But I won't let him get to me, I just won't.

Deimos looks at me for a long pause before he nods. "Come, I want to get cleaned up and take you away from everything for a while."

"I'd love that." He collects my hand and we slip out into the hallway and make our way to his room. "Thank you for helping back there."

His lips pinch to one side, and his hold just squeezes slightly. "No one is going to hurt you again."

I smile to myself because I never expected to have men in my life who cared and protected me so much.

Once in his chamber, he heads into his bath-room where I hear the splashing of water.

Unlike my room, Deimos has a huge bed, a couch, fireplace, even a table, all in the main area. It's twice as big as mine.

Deimos emerges, wiping his hand on a towel

while wearing nothing but dark pants that sit low on his hips. Muscles ripple across his chest and arms, his abs rock-hard with a thin line of hair trailing down into his pants. With everything happening so quickly since I arrived in this realm, with Deimos falling sick, we never got a chance to be together. The way he looks at me now is temptation on steroids, and my nipples pebble at the way his stare devours me.

"Come over here, kitten."

I involuntarily move toward him, my body now listening to him, apparently. I slide right into his arms, and he embraces me, nestling his face into the curve of my neck. Each breath I take fills me with the masculine scent that is all Deimos and has me melting against him. Looping my arms around his chest, I know my heart is in a good place with him. It sounds corny, but after he collected me from Earth and all the things we went through, the cure and magic I used to heal him, there's a bond between us.

"You always smell like delicious berries," he whispers in my ear, then draws my earlobe into his mouth with his tongue.

My toes curl in my boots, and every inch of me shivers with anticipation. This whole time, I've only kissed Deimos and done some heavy petting, but nothing more. Now, I can't get the image of us naked and together out of my mind. I crave it, long for it...

He lifts his head to look at me, and my attention goes to the cut under his eye. It's healed, even if blushing pink.

"How did you get that wound?" I ask, knowing he went out hunting yesterday. I skim my fingers underneath the wound lightly, then kiss his cheek.

"I want to say it was from a fight with a bear in the woods within the kingdom grounds, but the truth is we don't have anything wild in here. Only pheasants and deer. I tripped over a tree root and a low hanging branch whipped me in the face."

A laugh erupts past my lips and I regret it at once, but I can't stop myself. "I'm sorry, but that's hilarious."

He raises a brow, then his fingers find the bottom of my top and slide under to tickle my ribs.

I flinch and cry out as he tickles me like a mad man playing the piano. Slapping his hand, I shove him away playfully and leap out of his reach.

"Come back here, I'm not finished," he teases.

"Don't you dare or I'll scream. I'm ticklish."

His lips quirk upward. "I know." Then he lunges after me.

A yelp flies past my throat and I spin away, darting across the room. I jump up and scramble right over his bed, making a mess of it, then hop down, snatching a pillow for a weapon. Giddiness claims me; I can't remember the last time I just acted silly and laughed at nothing.

He comes at me, careening around the bedpost. I slap the pillow into his head, and he shoves it aside. Then in a flash, he swoops an arm under my knees and another around my back, swinging me up and off my feet.

"You cheat!" I declare.

"How is that cheating? I caught you and now I get to have my way with you."

I cling to his neck, pressing my lips to his collarbone. "There were no rules about this, so it doesn't apply."

He tosses me onto my back on the bed. The mattress bounces beneath me, and he crawls over me, making his way up from my legs to my face. "That's where you're wrong, my kitten. I always get my way, even if I have to play dirty."

I push myself up and reach for a pillow to whack him in the head, but he matches my attempt with a kiss. Our mouths come together; they mash, our tongues craving one another. He kisses me deeply and hungrily, and I don't blame him. This has been way too long in the making.

His hand reaches for my shirt, and he tugs at it aggressively, the buttons popping. He's so strong, all angles, and looks spectacular.

And in that split second of meeting his gaze, a memory I'd forgotten slams into me.

Every time I've kissed Deimos, my power shot outward and opened a portal. As if thinking the same thing, his eyes widen, and he gets off the bed in a heartbeat. His hand meets mine and he pulls me to my feet.

"Shit, did you open a portal again? Can you feel it?" Frantically, he scans the room like somehow the answer lays in here somewhere.

My mind is reeling at a hundred miles an hour, and for the life of me I can't remember if I even felt a surge of power. Arousal, yes, in bucketfuls. Power? Not sure.

"Guendolyn," he prompts me, holding onto my arms.

"Don't rush me. I'm trying to think. How could I forget about this? It only happens with you, not your brothers, but why?"

"So, you kissed my brothers while I was close to death in bed?" His brows pinch, his shoulders curving forward almost in a defeated pose.

I cock my brow at him. "Really? That's what bothers you right now? Anyway, I'm convinced there was no power energy when you and I just kissed," I state. His brow remains furrowed, and I can't tell what upsets him most. Me kissing his brothers or that I might have opened another portal somewhere.

"You sure?" He's already leaving my side and crossing the room in long strides, his arms swinging at his sides.

"Yes. Last time it was unmissable. There was no shaking of walls now."

He opens the door. "I'll be right back." And he's gone in seconds.

Oh, shit. Why can't things just be normal? Like kissing my boyfriend shouldn't always come with the potential of hell unleashed.

Deimos returns so fast, I haven't moved from where I stand. "My men are doing a sweep of the kingdom just to be on the safe side." He strolls closer. "So, you're certain you didn't feel any tingling of power."

The more I think about it, the more I'm positive. "Yes."

"Why? What's changed?"

The same thought crosses my mind, and I shrug, going through everything that happened recently. But with regards to controlling the portals, something has changed.

"Hmm, well actually." I reach down to my pocket and pull out the ruby.

"Is that fairy stone from the king's throne?"

"Yep. And when I hold it, I can now control opening a portal. So—"

"So that's the answer. It's got to be next to you." His hands settle on my hips and he tugs me toward him. "Thank fuck, as I can't take any more shit, especially if it means not taking you as mine."

I stare up into his gorgeous eyes, and the panic attack we both had fades. He guides me back to the bed and kisses me, softly this time. My arousal spikes in moments. Our mouths part, and I lean toward the dresser and place the stone down.

Deimos is right there, picking up the ruby and pressing it back into my hand. "Hold it just to be on the safe side." There's a serious tone in his voice, a worry that somehow I'll unleash another wave of disaster on the kingdom.

I can't even roll my eyes at his concern because last time we kissed, it ended in him being bitten by a Bloodcursed. I almost lost him, and the panic and danger we faced to save him is not something I want to experience again. Wrapping my fingers around the stone, I flop back onto the bed and call him to me with a bent finger.

My heart is racing, a flush flaring over me as I pull off the remainder of my top, along with the undergarment. Nipples pebbled from the sudden coldness, the anticipation of what's to come hums through me.

Deimos groans his approval as he stares down at me, the sound sending a spike of desire between my thighs. My prince leans over me, his lips on my breast, kissing it all around, making his way to the nipple. He accepts it greedily into his mouth, sucking on it like he's starved, like I'm the air he breathes and he can't get enough.

I moan against his touch, running my fingers through his long blond hair. He's captivating, everything I always wanted. I always thought men like him were not in my league—turns out I was wrong.

Closing my eyes, I soften into the mattress and feel every kiss, every mock bite, every lick as

Deimos adores my breasts. I wrap my legs around his hips, lifting my pelvis up to grind myself against the erection in his pants. The stone in my hands feels still cold.

When his mouth is on mine again, I flip open my eyes and wrap myself around him, kissing him back. I can't get enough of tasting his lips.

His hand dips between us and pops open my pants. My stomach flip-flops—I'm so horny and yet at the same time, slightly shy. I'm not the most practiced girl when it comes to sex, and well, this is our first time.

A sudden rapping on the door has us both freezing. We exchange worried looks.

"Must be my men," he murmurs before he jumps up to his feet and rushes across the room as I tug the blanket up to cover myself.

Please don't let there be a portal I'd opened. I love kissing Deimos, so universe, don't take that away from me.

I wrench open the door to my bedroom. Two of my guards stand in the hallway, and their faces show no traces of shock or terror. "Did you find anything?" I ask.

"Nothing. All is fine," Reinland says, the taller of the two.

"Are you certain?"

They both nod, and relief washes over me. Maybe Guendolyn was right that the fairy ruby controls her magic when she's with me. Though it begs the question... Why did my kiss trigger her power in the first place?

"Alright. Let me know if it changes," I instruct my guards and shut the door. My sexy kitten lies in my bed, wrapped up in the blankets, only her head poking out.

"Sounds like we're all clear," she says, climbing out of the nest she made for herself.

My gaze dips to her gorgeous bouncy breasts tipped with the most perfect rosy nipples. She sees me staring, and her cheeks blush. I love how easily she responds, how innocently she reacts when she's normally feisty. Both sides of the same coin, and I adore everything about her.

"I'm disappointed," I state. "You're still wearing your pants."

She grabs a pillow and tosses it at me. "You can't talk. Take off yours first."

I grin and march over to her as she draws another pillow to her chest.

"You're mine." I snatch the pillow from her grasp and throw it behind me. Then I grab her by the waist and haul her to me, my fingers tearing apart her buttons.

Her eyes widen. I let my arousal take the lead, and I hook my fingers into the top of her pants and yank them and her underwear down her legs.

She takes a deep gasp of surprise.

The pants jam at her ankles, as she's still

wearing her boots. I tsk, meeting her sheepish expression.

She shrugs and sticks her tongue out. "That's what happens when you rush."

I can't deny, I enjoy her fighting against me. As I reach down to grab her foot and rip off her boots, I take in her gorgeous body. Round breasts, her waist cinching in then beautifully curving to follow her hips. The small mound of light hair between her legs glistens, and already her arousal perfumes the air.

My cock twitches, growing. Frantically, I drag the boots and pants off so I can reach my girl.

"Don't make me wait too long," she teases me, her eyes batting as she lays there looking spectacular.

She looks at me with wide eyes, lips parted, her knees locked together as she lies on the bed, propped up on her elbows. My balls ache with a desperate need to claim what I've wanted for too fucking long.

I reach a hand down to her knees, and her breath quickens at my touch. I pry them open. She gives no resistance. Her sweet pussy is slick, and I run my thumb over the seam of her heat.

She trembles, her thighs falling wider. Her hips

rise slightly in response to my strokes. Unsure how much longer I can hold on, I lean forward and sweep my hand to the back of her neck and bring her up to kiss me.

Her gasp makes me want to protect her from the world.

"I missed you so much," she whispers, struggling for breath through her emotions.

"Today I will claim you, mark you, show you what you've missed." Let her see that no matter what the future holds, she will always have me by her side. To keep her in our kingdom, I may propose to my brothers that Luther or I marry her under the court's rule to avoid hiding her. We'll need to work out how to create her a Seelie identity, but I drive those thoughts aside.

I can't believe I just thought of marriage when I vowed to never settle down.

"Stop talking, just kiss me," she demands.

Her mouth melts against mine. She's soft and smells so good, and hell, all the things I want to do to her... We fit perfectly together, and I'm not just talking about sex. I intend to get to know her better, to show her life here can be magnificent with Luther and me by her side. I want to protect her, wrap her in my arms and keep her close.

Her fingers thread through my long hair, drawing me closer. Need claws through me, and our mouths part. Her cheeks and lips are rosy, and the heat in her eyes calls to me.

"Take me," she says, and my cock twitches at her words.

I lay her back on the bed and pull back, tugging my pants down my legs and stepping out of them. My erection sits stiff and so hard it aches.

"Touch it," I ask, and my kitten obliges, sitting up, her lower lip between her teeth, gaze locked on my cock. She grasps the shaft, and I hiss at the sensation. Her long fingers curl all the way around, and she tugs.

"Fuck!" I've waited for this so damn long.

Soft wetness presses around my tip, and I glance down to that sweet cherry mouth wrapped around my cock.

My chest rises and falls quicker, my blood racing south, balls tightening.

Oh, hell! My eyes flutter upward as she takes me deeper and deeper. That wicked tongue lashes over my erection, the sensation driving me insane. I rock my hips forward and back, slowly at first, but the intensity escalates too fast.

I slip out of her mouth with a pop, and she

simply looks up at me with doe eyes. She kneels on the edge of the bed, naked and spectacular. I can't stop focusing on her perky breasts, the way her waist draws in, the small thatch of light hair between her legs. I need more. So much more.

"Lay on your back, kitten," I order, and she slips down onto her side, untucking her legs and laying back. "Show me everything again, wider so I can see those glistening lips."

Her breaths quicken and she lifts her legs, widening her bent knees. "I love when you talk like this to me," she purrs.

I fall before her, staring at the pink slit, her arousal so obvious. My dick twitches.

Kissing her inner thigh, I make my way higher. Her sexy, musky scent is intoxication. I take it deep into my lungs, arising a primal hunger inside me. Before I even reach her juicy lips, she moans.

I groan at the sight of her spread before me. Then I flick out a tongue and lick her length. She arches her back, her legs widening, giving me everything she has. Taking her into my mouth, I suck on her and ravage what is mine.

"Oh, fuck! Deimos!" she screams.

She's so wet, her pelvis rocking back and forth.

I devour my sweet kitten, wanting her so close to the edge she'll beg me for more.

I tongue her, my fingers gripping her hips as I shove myself deeper, pinning her to me.

Her cries of pleasure rile me up; they make me so fucking horny, holding back is killing me.

I pull back as she cranes her head up to look at me. "Why are you stopping?

Up on my feet, I laugh, because this is how I want her. Spread open, craving me. "Neither of us are going anywhere, kitten." I cover my body over hers and our mouths clash. My cock presses to the heat between her thighs, finding the place I need to bury myself into. She's an addiction I can't get enough of.

Taking her tongue into my mouth, I push my dick into her. She adjusts her hips, making it easier to slide inside. She's tight, her walls clenching, and holding back grows harder.

"Let me in, angel," I breathe against her. "Just relax, I won't hurt you."

She nods, and I physically feel her softening.

I growl as I slide in all the way, my heart pounding.

"Deimos," she cries.

I pull out and go back in, slow at first so she

adjusts to my size, then I move faster. Fucking her, pumping.

Her breasts rub against my chest with each thrust, her eyes never leaving mine. I adore the way she moans, how her body responds to me, curling around me like we are one.

"This feels so right," she says. "I missed you."

I kiss her, never stopping myself from burying my cock in her. With one hand sliding between us, I reach for her clit and rub it.

Her breaths rush and she moans against my mouth.

"Come for me, kitten," I whisper, then dip my head lower and grab her nipple between my teeth. I gnaw on it gently, then suck on it.

Her breaths labor, and in a heartbeat, her body shudders beneath me. She cries out, convulsing with the orgasm tearing through her.

Her pussy squeezes my cock, and I let myself go this time, rip open the floodgates as I explode inside her. I growl, pulsing, feeding her my seed, both of us gasping for air.

Clasping the bedsheets, her head tilts back with her beautiful screams of pleasure. Fuck, she's gorgeous.

By the end when we're both floating down, I press my mouth to hers softly. "I want more."

She breaks out laughing, then cups my face and kisses me. "Yes, please."

I draw out of her and push up to my feet. Her pussy glistens, her lips full, and I fucking love seeing the white seep of my seed at her entrance.

"I'll get something to clean you."

She winks and stays there. Her hand outstretches and she opens the fist holding her ruby. "I feel like this stone should have been with me all along. I mean, I can open and close portals with it—though I'm not sure yet I can control where I'll end up—but it's an improvement. And well, I can kiss you to my heart's content."

"I need to find a solution so you don't have to grasp it each time I want to kiss you."

"I'd love that," she answers from the bed.

In the bathroom, I collect a towel and moisten it slightly at one end, then return to my kitten. I clean her delicious pussy, then I climb into bed with her, taking her into my arms.

"This is how our future is going to be. Freedom to be together, to share our lives."

She's curled up against my chest, face to face, then she glances up at me. "It's strange how I feel more at home here than I ever did back on Earth."

"That tells you everything," I muse.

"I really thought I'd lose you," she begins, her hand on my bicep trembling.

"You risked so much for me, and I don't doubt for a moment how much you feel for me. But promise me you won't ever put yourself into such danger for me again."

She scrunches her nose like she'll never do that, and it doesn't surprise me.

"If I didn't go to Ash Court, I never would have discovered so much."

"Oh yeah?" I massage her lower back, encouraging her to tell me more.

"Like meeting the king's mother; finding out that my mother must be important, whoever she is; or that I have more power inside me than I first thought. Plus, I never would have bumped into Hiss to get the ruby. And then, then there's who my real—"

"Hiss?" I query, and she gives me a quick rendition of what happened while I was sick, and I merge it with what my brothers told me. "The fairy with blue wings, right?"

She nods. "But there's something else." She

swallows hard, and I see the trepidation in her expression.

"What is it?"

A pounding knock erupts at the door, and she flinches in my arms.

"Let me see who that is. Get under the blankets."

I drag on my pants and stride across the room. Once Guendolyn is covered, I open the door.

My guard stands before me, his gaze never drifting into my room. "You've been summoned by His Highness, Prince Ahren, to his meeting room immediately."

I groan and run a hand through my hair. What the hell now? With a quick nod, I reply, "I'll be there shortly." Then I close the door and turn to my kitten, who again has only her head sticking out from under the blanket in my bed.

"Stay here." I close the distance between us and lean over her, then kiss those full lips. "I'll be back later and bring you some food."

"Sounds like a plan. Don't be long." She snuggles deeper under the blanket like she might go to sleep.

My heart thumps in my chest. What has she done to me?

Fuck!

She's constantly on my mind, and my cock hardens just at the thought of her. I should have known from the first time I went to collect her from Earth she'd captivate me. I insisted my job was just to bring her to Shadow Court, but I'd been fooling myself.

She had always been mine. I just had to admit it to myself.

CHAPTER 7

GUENDOLYN

Islide into the scorching hot water before reaching over for grapes from the platter of fruit near the tub while the morning sun shines gloriously. Yesterday, after a while when Deimos hadn't returned, a maid delivered my early dinner in the room. After which I crashed on the bed and slept all the way through. Deimos still wasn't in my bed this morning so I decided to get on with the day, starting with a wash.

I made my way down to the baths because I can't wait around doing nothing.

My guard waits for me outside, and right now it's better I stay low. The princes are most likely talking about the king's funeral, about Ahren taking the throne, so I can wait.

Though it keeps playing on my mind about the king being my real father, and how much I desperately wanted to tell Deimos. But I feel selfish doing so.

The throne is Ahren's, even if he's not the king's son by blood. And if I announce this now, will I come across as someone trying to steal the throne from him? In all honesty, I don't know enough about royal rules and politics to know if that's possible. Can a female take a throne in fae courts?

Regardless, I don't want such a position, and I'm already so close to losing Ahren. I won't do anything to jeopardize pushing him even farther from me.

A stupid thought pops into my mind, one of marriage, and I almost laugh out loud. Right, a court that hates Unseelie will never allow one to rule over them. Even if only half an Unseelie, I don't really belong in their court, now do I? And technically, it means the princes and I are step-siblings.

Nope, I'm not even going there. There is no bloodline shared between us.

It's why I contemplated asking Deimos' opinion, but is that a smart decision? What's to stop him from making a big deal of this and telling Ahren?

I slip deeper into the water, deciding to say nothing for now.

Sucking in a deep breath, I relax and think about the incredible time with Deimos and how I don't know what I'd do if I lost him and Luther. It shocks me how quickly they've grown on me. I let myself linger on those thoughts and not what I'm losing.

When the water temperature falls and my fingers resemble prunes, I climb out of the tub and grab a towel. The maids had taken my clothes and left me with a dress. I pick up the deep blue fabric pebbled with tiny crystals and find no underwear. I sigh, tired of going around with no panties. Is this a fae thing?

What I miss desperately are slack pants and a hoodie. These gowns may look spectacular, lift my breasts, cinch in my waist, but they aren't uber comfortable.

Dressed, I pull on the square neckline that sits a bit too low over my chest, then tie up the laced corset across the front, squishing my breasts together. No need for a bra when the ladies are constantly pressed inside a corset or tight dress.

Stepping into a pair of ankle boots, I run the wide-toothed comb through my hair. Then I head into the hall.

Michae greets me with a smile, standing taller. He has a healed cut on his upper lip that only reveals itself when he grins. He's growing on me, and it's nice to have someone to talk to. "Where to, Miss?"

"The dining hall, please. I'm thirsty." He nods, and we head through the mansion.

Two maids rush past us, holding their skirts for ease. I glance back to see them vanish around a corner. A man in a black suit pushing a silver food trolley races down the corridor, coming toward us.

He waves a hand for us to get out of the way.

We do, and he's a storm, exploding past us.

"What's going on?" I mumble to myself.

More maids carrying baskets of fruit dart past. Another woman behind them has her arms filled with flowers. Then two men roll more trolleys piled high with beautiful gold plates. Their rattling sounds have me cringing as I picture them falling over and smashing.

I blink at the commotion down every hallway. "What are they preparing for? The funeral?"

"His highness Ahren is set take the throne in a few days."

"So this is for a celebration then?"

When Dana marches past us with bundles of linen in her arms, I reach out for her, stepping in her path.

She bows and darts past, the older man huffing and vanishing into a room.

"Guess it's not every day a new king is crowned," I murmur. Of course, I don't expect to be invited, though I do hope Deimos or Luther sneak me in. I want to see the throne room decorated elaborately, to witness the ritual and party to understand fae culture. To see if they are anything like medieval festivities in movies.

Leaving behind the commotion, we enter the dining room in the mansion. The beautiful wall of windows always draws my attention to the ocean of trees and mountains. This has to be one of my favorite rooms.

"I'll request a drink for you," Michae states and heads through the back door that leads into the kitchen.

Returning my attention to the window, I glance out there and try not to overthink all the commotion that makes me feel like I'm being left out. This isn't about me, I keep telling myself.

Footsteps close in behind me, and I turn, expecting Michae, except it's Luther. Where did he come from?

My chest swells with the way his mouth spreads into a delicious grin. His dark hair is swept off his face, and his cheeks glow like he's been outside in the cold. The black tunic he wears hugs his strong chest and broad shoulders, gold dots embroidering the round neckline. A leather belt sits loosely around his waist, and his leather pants hug muscular thighs. His boots are speckled with snow, confirming my suspicion.

"I've been searching for you," he says, taking my hand in his and drawing me toward him. "I have a surprise."

"What is it?" I can't help but grin widely, lapping up the attention he gives me.

"You'll see."

Just then, Michae emerges carrying a glass of juice and places it on the long dining table for me.

"Order the chef to arrange a packed feast for me. We don't have much time to wait," Luther orders.

The guard taps his chest just over his heart

twice. "Of course, Your Highness." Then he returns to the kitchen.

Luther looks devilishly handsome today, and I love how his greedy fingers hold onto me, never letting me get far from him.

"Did you just come out of the meeting with Deimos and Ahren?" I ask, curious about what they discussed and if it had anything to do with finding the king's killer.

"It dragged so long. They didn't even serve us lunch, and I'm starved. Deimos will most likely find his way here soon. He eats like a lion."

"And Ahren?" I query.

He slides strands of hair caught in my eyelashes behind my ear, and something crosses his gaze. Is it pity? Does he know Ahren pushed me aside, that now I pine for him? I hate myself for coming across that way, but I can't control how I feel about these princes.

"He's busy," Luther explains. "He'll be busy for a few weeks, at least." His hand falls to my lower back and nudges me to the table. "Come, let's sit as we wait."

But I don't budge from my spot. "Is that how long crowning a king takes?"

He swallows loud, his Adam's apple bobbing up

and down his throat. He hesitates, and it only strengthens my suspicion that there is so much more going on here. Why am I being kept in the dark?

"Luther, what's going on with Ahren? Why is he turning away from me?" I don't want to bring this up here and now, but the way he stares at me draws my emotions to the surface. I fell hard for three princes, but in truth, I'm still getting to know them. Still discovering their secrets. So what exactly is Ahren's?

Luther licks his lips, looking like he's deciding what to tell me. "He needs to talk to you himself. I'm sorry, little wolf. I'm surprised he hasn't, but I'll mention it to him."

My stomach drops and hits the ground. Just great. So there *is* something beyond him having extra responsibility or whatever else he insisted. They were lies.

Now my mind spins with horrible scenarios, like he's sick and going to die, or he needs to go live across the realm for years as part of taking the throne, or... god, I need to stop torturing myself.

"Little wolf, you will always have me and Deimos by your side."

Why does he keep saying that? I pull from him

and turn to the window, wishing more than anything I had wings like a bird and could fly out there. To feel free and not be so confused and trapped.

In this realm, I'm the stranger.

The foreigner who is vulnerable and gullible.

I rely on the princes, and I hate that. I see that now, because they can walk away just as easily as Ahren is. Where does that leave me?

Luther stands at my back but doesn't hold me. The heat from his body engulfs me like a warm blanket.

"Why can't you tell me what's going on with Ahren? I hate this. I don't even know where I belong. I keep getting brushed aside, needing to hide who I am. Is that who I will be? The person swept away when things get too real?" Anger and frustration tighten around my throat.

Luther takes my shoulders and spins me to face him. My back presses against the glass window, and I glance up at him.

"That's not fair, little wolf. We have to keep you safe until we find a way to make your stay here more permanent. I've told you before that I'll do anything to protect you, and you need to trust me, now more than ever."

There's truth in his warm eyes. I glance down, feeling heat in my face, loathing that I sound like a spoiled brat. "I just feel lost," I whisper.

His finger glides under my chin and lifts my head so I meet his gaze. He's inches from me, his expression heartfelt, his scent musky and spicy and so delicious. "You'll never be lost at my side."

His words are like a fresh spring breeze chasing away the winter blues, and my eyes prick. I melt against him, and he embraces me. I don't even know why I'm crying, but all the emotions building inside me finally rush out. The news of my father. Not knowing who my mother is. Ahren pushing me aside. Not knowing where I belong. And who exactly am I, anyway? Am I better off back on Earth where I'm nobody and I can pretend I have a life?

Luther rubs my back and holds me close. There's something about him that always calms me. Maybe because I've known him the longest. He's seen the worst and best sides of me and still sticks around. For those reasons, I embrace what he offers and believe him when he says he'll always be by my side.

Luther

My heart hurts.

From what I've seen, Guendolyn has faced challenge after challenge, and she always fights back. She's never once demanded to leave.

Not my little wolf.

She doesn't give up, I see that now. Her eagerness to uncover the truth of her past drives her, and I admire that more than she'll ever realize. Too many fall complacent, retreat from fear... but not her.

I embrace her as she softly sobs against my chest. Running my hand over her blonde hair, I don't rush her but let her settle down in her own time. We all need to regroup and reassess our next decisions when all hell breaks loose, and while her way of dealing is crying, mine is smashing anything in my way. Similar, in a way.

The heat from the fireplace engulfs us, while outside the sun peeks out from behind the clouds. The snowfall fades, as do the gray clouds.

This is what she needs. Time away from everything. Because once she finds out about the wedding, she will be heartbroken. Until then, I intend to make her smile so she has something to hold onto.

Guendolyn breaks from my embrace, her cheeks rosy, eyes still puffy.

"Change of scenery and fresh air, how does that sound?" I offer.

Her sweet lips curl upward as she nods. "I would love that." It warms me to see her smile rather than cry.

The maid appears from the kitchen, followed by Michae. She hands me a wicker basket covered by a white kitchen towel, and I feel like a servant about to stroll through the woods. But I take it nonetheless from her hand.

"Everything you need is in there, Your Highness." She bows her head slightly and retreats.

"Thank you," I say, and Guendolyn gives her thanks too. Michae bows his head as we leave the dining hall.

By the time we head downstairs and step outside into a courtyard, the expression on my little wolf's face is bursting with excitement.

"Where are we going?" She looks at me for an answer, and there is something riveting about her childlike enthusiasm. My chest tightens as my heart pounds for her. She affects me so easily, so quickly.

"You'll see," I assure her and guide her over the snow-covered yard to the large black sleigh harnessed to a large chestnut horse.

Guendolyn's mouth hasn't closed yet, and she quickens her steps. "Is this really for us? Oh my god, it looks like Santa's sleigh." She mumbles things I don't understand, but her excitement is contagious. Then she turns to me abruptly. "Wait, the Bloodcursed are outside the walls."

"Who said anything about leaving the kingdom grounds?"

She's bouncing on her feet and runs ahead, then climbs up into the open sleigh. She flops down onto the two-seater wooden bench covered in blankets, laughing when she looks my way.

"Hurry up," she calls.

This is how I want her to feel every day. Who would have thought I'd end up such a love-struck sucker. I need my little wolf by my side, always. That's what matters. I reach her and set the basket under the bench in the sleigh and turn to find our stable manager, an older fae with long pointy ears sticking over messy white hair, marching over to me.

"Your Highness, you are all set to go. The paths have been cleared of snow." There's a glint in his eyes just like the maid's and Michae's as he glances over to Guendolyn and back at me. I can't help but get the impression the staff at the mansion are excited for me to be with her. Or maybe it's hopeful thinking on my part.

"Thank you."

Beyond the castle and town and within the kingdom walls lies a woodland safe from Blood-cursed, where fae can hunt game and pick wild fruit and vegetables.

I climb into the sleigh, take the reins, and sit next to my little wolf. "Are you ready?"

"You bet. I'm so excited to do something fun. I still remember the Ferris Wheel you made for me." She presses up against my side, and I wrap an arm around her.

The horse takes off, and she bursts out giggling as we lurch backwards in our seat. We quickly fall into a steady trot, going over small bumps over the terrain. A few maids wave to us from the grounds, and Guendolyn repays the favor. Once we leave behind the castle yard, we start moving faster. I swing the horse right and take the path where pines and firs stripped of leaves and pine needles fill the landscape.

Behind us lays another path that leads into the Seelie Shadow town, but today I want us away from everyone and the fucking drama of royal life.

We jostle in our seat, but Guendolyn doesn't dislodge herself from my side. "When I was young," I begin, "I used to go into these woods and stay out here for a week at a time. I'd camp out here, catch my own meals and build fires, and I usually only returned when one of my brothers came to collect me."

"Escape?" she asks.

Sort of. A faint tingle of energy brushes over my skin, like it always does when I send her my thoughts.

She looks up at me, and it's strange to sense her emotions while also seeing them dance across her face. That's part of my ability… I may not clearly hear all of her response, but I do pick up on her feelings when she opens her mind to me. And right now, she's beyond curious.

I beat her to the questioning as we head through the woods, jumping about in our seat from the bumpy land. "My second sight came from my grandfather on my father's side. When we first moved to Shadow Court, I struggled to shut out the thoughts of people who had no idea how to guard their minds. You'd be surprised what people give away if I prod just enough. And I was young, still unable to control my power. So I used to hide here where I could keep my mind silent."

"Didn't your grandfather teach you to manage your power?"

I stare straight ahead at the path that starts to curve right and upward. Snow covers everything in sight, reminding me of the last time I saw my grandfather. A week before my tenth birthday, he'd entered my father's mind a few too many times to steal guarded information. When my father caught him, he killed my grandfather for it. Knowledge is power and makes people gruesome beings.

"Not really," I answer. "He wasn't the friendliest or most helpful fae." Which was the truth. He used to beat our real father as a child until he was bloody. Guess the whole apple not falling far from the tree applied here since Ahren was then treated the same. But the three of us made a pact to never become our father. And if we started down that road, we pulled each other back on track.

"That's a shame." She loops her arms tighter

around my middle and nestles closer. "It seems to me you have it down pat if you were able to track me down on Earth."

"With the use of magic," I remind her.

"Still, what you can do is incredible."

I lean down and kiss the top of her head. "Says the girl who can open portals and heal fae, not to mention communicate with fairies."

"I think I have another ability," she tells me and goes on to explain about the energy she used to combat the king's mother in Ash Court.

My heart jackhammers at hearing she used energy to drive the Unseelie across the room. "You are incredible, my little wolf. And part of me wonders if you may even make a good mage."

She stiffens and pulls back. "Don't even say that. I've seen the mages in this court, and they are terrifying. I am nothing like that."

"You're right, you're different, and this is why I vow to protect you with my life."

She smiles and buries her head against me as we make our way forward. Birds chirp, and a deer darts past our path. Finally, I guide our horse to a stop in a small clearing where the white snow on the ground looks untouched. It glistens under the sun that's warmed up the icy day.

"We're going on foot from here. I have something to show you. Bring a blanket to keep you warm."

I jump out of the carriage and help her down as she holds onto the blanket from the bench. As she wraps it around her shoulders, I quickly give the horse feed to keep him content while we're gone.

Hand in hand, Guendolyn and I trek through the ankle-deep snow, walking past trees and over logs, the land sloping upward sharply.

She's gasping for air. "Are you trying to kill me?"

I laugh and draw her closer to me, helping her up the steep terrain to ensure she doesn't slip. Trees grow thinner, the sun stronger, and I love it up here. Around us, the world seems farther away, smaller; it feels like nothing can touch us.

We rise over the treetops now, following the circular path around the rocky hill. Once we reach the flat platform on the summit, I glance out to Shadow Court. Lofty and dominating over the land, the castle is ancient, stones worn from centuries of wear. Walls rise from the ground and stand protective over the kingdom with steadfast towers to watch over them. The town surrounds it, homes covering the descending landscape. And snow covers everything in sight.

"Oh my god!" Guendolyn gasps at the sight. "It's stunning up here. I need a camera because this is crazy beautiful."

"Little wolf, that view is not what I brought you up here for. Turn around."

She does, and her mouth drops open. "Are you freaking kidding me?"

CHAPTER 8

GUENDOLYN

Standing on a hill in the woods behind the castle, I stare out into the far distance, over the kingdom wall and another great expanse of woodland. My sight settles on an enormous tree I've never seen before. It towers over the woods around it as though someone placed a skyscraper in the middle of nowhere.

From our position on top of the hill, I can't make out the smaller details, only the branches tangled around the trunk, shooting upward where the canopy springs outward like an oversized mushroom top.

Hundreds of tiny lights speckle along the branches like fireflies.

"So beautiful," I murmur. "What is that tree?"

"Take a closer look." Luther hands me a pair of black binoculars that definitely did not come from this world.

I peer through them, my eyes taking a moment to work out what I'm looking at. Then I lower them because I've been staring at the sky. I zoom over to the tree that glints in the sunlight. The leaves sparkle like jewels, and from the branches hang oversized beehives.

My heart skips a beat as the realization hits me that I've seen these before. After we stepped out of the portal when escaping Ash Court.

"Holy shit! Those are fairies' homes!" I lower the binoculars and turn to Luther, who's grinning ridiculously.

"Why didn't you tell me they lived so close to the castle?" I swing back around to stare at a fairy emerging from a hive, her wings spanning outward in brilliant reds and golds. There are so many of these gorgeous fairies, all buzzing about like bees, popping in and out of the homes and then vanishing into the canopy tops. "We need to come here at night. Can you imagine how stunning this will look?" I lower the binoculars and glance over at Luther. "Can we go there?"

"If anyone gets near the tree, they attack and

kill them. Even the Bloodcursed are afraid. Many fear and hunt them down to ensure they don't swarm the kingdom. We're under a kind of unspoken agreement that we each stay on our side of the land." He gives me a wonky smile, almost awkward, almost apologetic.

"They are super protective of their homes. I don't blame them." I turn my attention back in the tree's direction, taken aback by the beauty this realm holds. I think back to the stories I've been told about the fairy queen, the tragedy she encountered, the history behind the fairies' existence. The reactions from fae when fairies are mentioned, including the princes.

They are feared.

But also misunderstood.

I think of Hiss and how she helped me, of the hundreds of fairies that bowed and sang to me. Those are not the actions of a wild, vicious race. They are trying to survive in this terrifying world that hunts them down, exploits them. They are direct descendants from the fairy queen herself, pushed aside by the Unseelie and Seelie alike. I recall the Ash King's mother gloating about her bloodline being directly linked to the fairies. Then why don't they embrace them into their court?

My mind runs rampant with injustice.

Luther closes in behind me, his hard chest pressed against my back as his arms wrap around my waist. His breath is on my neck. "To answer your earlier question, it's only after our recent trip that I realized how closely connected you are to them. They recognize you as one of their own."

The reality of his words is too much, except deep down in my gut, I know it's true. From the first time I encountered them, they saved me. One of them talked to me in my mind. One word, but still—communication.

"Are the fairies known for having abilities other than devouring the flesh from a person's bones in seconds?" I ask.

"Not that I'm aware of, though the fairy queen carried incredible power. She tapped into elemental magic, the legends say. It's why fae have such a varying array of powers. But most have been diluted over the generations."

The more I discover about this realm's history and inhabitants, the more it starts to piece together and somehow seem normal to me.

"I like the fairies," I admit.

"Yes, I know," he answers and kisses my cheek. Warmth spreads over my body from his affection.

Twisting my head, I glance back at him, but he surprises me, sliding a hand across my jaw and kisses me.

Powerful and intoxicating, he knows exactly how to distract me and make me forget about what I'd been thinking about seconds earlier.

When he breaks away, I melt my back against his chest and hold onto his arms locked around me.

"I knew the first time I found you that there was something special about you," he muses.

"Well, of course. I was the girl with a curse," I answer with sarcasm.

His hold squeezes lightly around me. "Not what I meant. When I enter someone's mind, I can feel their aura. I can't explain it, but I sense in my heart how pure their soul is, and you are untouched."

"Untouched?" I turn around in his arms to face him.

"Nothing stains your soul. Everyone has some level of corruption or darkness in their aura. It's part of who we are. Except you. I've never seen that before."

I open my mouth, but nothing comes out. I'm unsure what to ask.

He cups my cheeks and kisses my nose. "I think

it means you are destined for something unimaginable."

"That sounds terrifying." My breath quickens. "I have yet to see when anything in this realm is filled with butterflies and rainbows rather than death and blood."

"These hardships will shape your legacy, little wolf."

I half-laugh at the motivational quote. "You are confusing me with someone else. Everyone wants me killed."

He leans in closer and whispers in my ear, "You got that backward, beautiful. Anyone with a death warrant is direly important. Even if you don't realize it yet."

I frown and tilt back my head to look at him. "Do you know something I don't? Tell me; don't talk in circles, please. I've had enough of secrets."

"You are special, that part is obvious. Exactly why or how is still unclear, but it doesn't take anything away from you."

When his mouth grazes mine, I press myself against him and kiss him, tired of the merry-go-round conversations that leave me uncomfortable. I've never been anyone important, and I refuse to believe that somehow that has changed. I've experienced enough to know how the universe works. When it gives me something good in my life, it usually comes with a sucker punch. And I just feel like I haven't felt its full brunt yet. Luther telling me otherwise is his way of distracting me, to placate me.

With no answers, I prefer not to talk about this anymore.

I focus on how amazing Luther tastes instead, how his hands slide to my ass, fingers digging into me with a possessiveness I adore.

On my first time in this realm, I kissed Luther up in the treetops, so it fits perfectly that we find ourselves high up on a hill, overlooking the land, in each other's arms.

An icy breeze washes past, ruffling my hair and tugging on my clothes. Luther holds me closer, our lips still crushed together.

"I'll take you back to the sleigh. The winds are too harsh up here." His face is so close to mine, our noses touch.

I still struggle to believe that I somehow caught his attention. If it wasn't for this wind, I'd insist we remain right where we are.

He takes my hand, and I race alongside him down the slope, staring out to the fairy tree one last time before it vanishes from sight behind tree-tops and the lofty kingdom wall.

By the time I climb back into the sleigh, my teeth are chattering, and the first feathery snowflakes cascade around us. Then it changes in the blink of an eye. Snow falls in thick sheets, the cold penetrating through to my core. I tuck the binoculars beneath our bench and touch the basket.

"We didn't eat our picnic meal," I remind him.

"It won't go to waste, trust me." Luther slides in next to me, wrapping an arm around my shoulders and gripping the reins, then we are traveling through the woods again.

"The weather changed so fast." The earlier blue sky is now bruised with dark stormy clouds, darkening the woodland.

I rub my arms and curl in closer against Luther, absorbing his heat, though my nose still feels like ice.

The trees blanketed in snow blur past us as we move faster, and with the snow coming down quickly, I can barely see the track ahead of us, let alone anything else. Branches swing wildly in the blizzard, the wind howling around us.

My heart is beating with the thought that somehow we'll get stuck out here in the storm.

"Keep your head low," Luther instructs.

That's when I feel the ice pellets bounce off the blanket around my shoulders and my head.

A sudden gust of freezing air rushes past, colliding into us, throwing us back into our seats.

"Oh shit!" I gasp, and I won't deny, I'm more than a bit scared at how horrible the weather has shifted.

Luther whistles and drives our poor horse forward, then swings down a path toward the right. We're bouncing in our seat, and I can't stop shivering.

Before us, a small wooden cottage materializes through the curtain of snow.

A sharply pointed roof, windows covered by curtains, and a small covered veranda at the front door.

"Where are we?" I raise my voice over the blustery weather.

"Hunter's lodge. It's always open for anyone stuck out here during a storm." He comes to a pause a small distance away. "Run inside, and I'll be there soon. I need to take the horse into the stable in the back."

I nod, already climbing up as I grab the basket from under the bench, then I jump out of the sleigh. My feet sink into the snow instantly.

Not wasting a second, I hug myself, tucking my chin into my chest and shoving against the wind to the front door. I look back as Luther ushers the horse and sleigh around the side of the hunter's lodge.

Quickly, I stamp my feet on the veranda to get rid of excess snow and push open the unlocked door, rushing inside.

It smells stale in here. I shut the door, pushing it against the ferocious gusts that whistle outside, closing it with a thump. I'm trembling and hurry to pull back the curtains to light up the dark room.

It's a spacious room with an enormous fireplace. Table and chairs near the door, a couch facing the fireplace, and a bed covered in furs in the back corner. I move forward and find another door, behind which lies a makeshift toilet. Basically a bench with a hole in it. At least it's not outside, so for that I'm glad. I close that door and make my way to the fireplace and the large stack of wood neatly piled against the wall.

I place a handful into the fireplace, but with no idea on how to start a fire without matches, I turn to the basket of food instead. Underneath the kitchen towel is an array of breads, sliced roast meat, cheeses, chutney, bottles of wine and water, and what looks like half a fruit cake. I lay them out on the table, finding not only plates, cups, and cutlery at the bottom, but also strips of cured meat, tomatoes, eggs I assume are hard boiled, and a small jar of churned butter along with a small bowl of tiny pears and plums. I have no idea how the kitchen packed so much into the basket, but I couldn't be happier to have all this food while trapped here during the storm.

The door opens abruptly, and an explosion of winds rushes into the cottage. The cold finds me, digging claws into my flesh, and I'm shaking instantly.

Luther forces the door shut and shakes his head, sending snow in every direction.

"It's wild out there. We might be stuck here until it quiets down, little wolf." The way he says that isn't with any hint of worry, but more of excitement at us two being alone together. For that, I'm excited too.

"I'll get the fire started, you serve the food," he says and blows me a kiss. My knees soften at the gesture, my stomach flip-flopping. "I'm so fucking hungry right now," he murmurs.

"Then get your ass into gear," I throw back playfully and look over at the lack of fire.

He doesn't take long to ignite a blaze and have it burning. An orange glow lights up the room quickly. The windows rattle from the wild weather, small pellets of ice hitting the glass, but in here, it feels cozy and oh-so-right when I look over to Luther getting to his feet.

He's gorgeous. Built like a bear, and those amber eyes complement his midnight black hair.

My gaze trails over his muscles, at how tall he stands… and why in the world does a fae like him see anything in me? Truthfully, I suspect if we crossed paths in the street, he wouldn't even bat an eye my way. I am ordinary. He is a god and would have every woman stopping in her tracks to check him out.

What drew us together were the years we spent in each other's minds, talking to one another. I may not have realized it at the time, but I fell for Luther long ago. And I believe he feels the same about me.

He turns to the table with the food. At the sight

of the mountain of food on his plate, my stomach groans.

I make my way toward the food and help myself before he eats it all—and that is no exaggeration.

We're both on the couch, enjoying our meal. With my legs folded under me, I balance the plate on the wide armrest. Heat from the fireplace curls around us, while the blaze crackles and spits. There's something therapeutic about eating comfort food and watching logs burning while a storm howls outside.

"If the weather doesn't stop, we'll spend the night here," Luther explains, then bites into a slice of roast venison. He watches me, waiting for my response like his comment is meant to elicit a dramatic reaction. Of course I know what he's implying. One bed, two of us.... and the thought sends a shiver of excitement down my spine.

I shrug and keep eating, refusing to show him my reaction. Mostly to tease the hell out of him. "How far is the castle anyway? Can't be that far."

He eyes me while I get up to fetch some cake. "You want to go back already?"

His gaze sits heavy on my back, and it takes

everything I have to refrain from grinning as I walk past him. He's so easy to rile up, it's hilarious.

The floorboard creaks behind me, and his hands are on my waist instantly. His breath is in my ear. "You're not as clever as you think you are, little wolf."

Setting the plate down on the table, I turn, but he forces me to remain with my back to him.

"Yeah, how do you figure?"

His mouth is on my neck, nipping at my skin, then licking up to my earlobe. My knees wobble. He ignites desire within me in seconds. That's all it takes, apparently.

"Because the moment you heard we are staying here tonight, your stomach fluttered and your delicious little pussy pulsed, didn't it?"

I scoff for effect. "If you say so."

His hands fall to my waist, fingers tugging at my pants. "Let's find out, shall we?" he teases.

I slap his hands away playfully and throw myself out of his arms, then pivot around to face him. "Don't even think about it." I poke my tongue out at him.

His expression morphs into one of mischief, clearly seeing my response as a challenge. God, I love that response more than I thought, and the idea of him chasing after me is exhilarating.

He lunges after me, and I spin and dart across the room, but there's hardly anywhere to go. Careening around the couch only brings him leaping over the furniture and straight for me.

I'm giggling as I whip around.

Strong arms snap around my middle and lift me off my feet.

"You're cheating." I love toying with him.

He laughs in my ear, his tone full of mirth. "Only the loser would say that."

I writhe against him. I'll show him who the loser is. But suddenly, I'm flying toward the bed and land face first on the soft mattress where I bounce up and down before settling. Hastily, I roll over, but Luther is there, forcing me back onto my stomach. His body covers mine, holding me in place. Butterflies burst through my stomach, the heat between my legs melting into a puddle.

"You know how long I've waited to have you all to myself?"

"Years," I gasp with sarcasm from under his weight.

He shifts to hold himself on bent arms, still on top of me. "The tiny taste I had in that small town was just the beginning. I haven't been able to get you out of my mind."

"And is squishing me to death part of your plan?"

He gently sweeps my long hair off the back of my neck, and his lips on my skin cover me in goosebumps. "If it means pinning you down."

His weight lifts off me in seconds, and he tugs the fabric of my dress up to my waist, exposing my bare ass.

"Oh, little wolf. Here you are protesting, and yet you've come prepared."

Heat scales my cheeks, and I roll over. "For your information, the maids took my underwear and never brought it back. Then you wanted to go on a sleigh ride, and well, here we are."

His eyebrows rise, as do the corners of my mouth. He tugs on his top and yanks it up and over his head, so he's bare-chested. "Yes, here we are." He grabs my ankles and drags me across the bed toward him.

I cry out with laughter, while hunger sweeps over his expression. "Tonight, you're mine."

CHAPTER 9

GUENDOLYN

’m burning up, and I'm still clothed.

Well, partially. Luther is only in his pants, and I'm missing my underwear. While I lay on my back on the bed, propped up on my elbows, I can't stop looking at my gorgeous fae. At the way his biceps flex as he runs a hand through his pitch-black hair, the pecs on his chest, the rippled abs. I could very well be staring at a model, except he's a prince and here for me. After everything we've been through, I still need to pinch myself to realize I'm in a relationship with this man.

I don't fully understand the exact level of our dating or courting…. It just happened.

Luther unbuckles his belt, and my gaze dips.

"I could watch you strip all day long," I tease.

"My preference is the other way around." A devious expression sweeps behind his eyes. "Once things settle down in the kingdom, we will announce to everyone we are officially together."

My body tingles at the promise of his words, but they also have me curious. "Like in telling everyone we're dating?"

"Huh?"

"Boyfriend and girlfriend kind of thing?" I sound like a thirteen-year-old, even to myself.

He nods. "If that is what you call it on Earth, then yes, we will announce to everyone that you and I are betrothed for the sake of rules. This way, no more hiding, and you can easily be with us."

My heart stops, and I push myself to sit up on the bed, crossing my legs. "What?" I suddenly can't speak, and my heart is racing at a million miles an hour.

"It's only to ensure that no one questions your presence in the mansion. And we can arrange for you to marry us as that is permitted."

My entire body is strung so tight. One second ago I thought he was proposing our engagement, and now he's implying it's going to be fake. Does that mean he doesn't want that? My head hurts, especially since this never crossed my mind until now. I adore the guys more than anything, and it kills me that I don't understand what is going on with Ahren. But I don't want to lose them, and I guess that means eventually ending up together for life. My thoughts ramble endlessly, while my chest constricts.

He kneels on the mattress in front of me, still in his pants, and reaches over to cup my face with one hand. "Are you going to be sick? You've suddenly gone pale."

I swallow the thickness in my throat. "So, you don't want to be betrothed to me?" They aren't the words I intended to ask, or the conversation I expected us to have. My cheeks blush that I made such a presumption or put Luther on the spot.

At this point, all I want is to feel safe and keep the three princes with me. To feel their kisses, their touches, their bodies against mine. Yeah, it sounds simple and maybe greedy—the voice in my head reminds me of that constantly—but is it wrong to want happiness?

Luther's smile warms me, but I don't want to talk about this any longer. All I'm doing is setting myself up for disappointment. He takes my hand and guides me off the bed.

"Come with me," he instructs.

I follow him to the window across the room from us. The trees sway wildly in the storm, the snow coming down at an angle now, the wind whistling past.

"Look straight ahead down the path."

Squinting, I tilt my head to the side and catch a perfect tiny view of the castle—the tall towers, the ridged bridges, the arched windows—all smothered in snow. It reminds me of a snow globe.

"It's beautiful."

"Once Ahren takes the throne, Deimos and I will rule the Shadow Court with him, but there are rules that come with such roles. We can't be seen in public with females unless we are courting them with the intention to marry them."

My breath catches in my throat, and I can't turn around as he embraces me from behind. I don't know where this conversation is going, but my stomach is turning. I really can't take any more surprises or disappointments right now.

"Deimos and I have talked about this. We both agreed that to keep you close to us, you will be betrothed to us." His arms squeeze me slightly as he kisses the side of my face.

I blink and twist around in his arms. "So like, a fake engagement?"

He narrows his gaze at me. "Why fake?"

My head spins at what he's saying, and I don't want to jump at conclusions. "Does betrothed mean something else in this world than it does on Earth?"

"It means we have the intention to marry."

The cold shock of his response knocks the breath out of me. Except, I'm missing something. "So, we will pretend to be engaged for as long as…" I don't know how to continue that, because what happens next? I still don't know where I really live or belong.

"You will have a new identity, but this isn't pretend, little wolf."

I stare into his genuine expression, and my stomach twists into knots, my knees close to giving out under me.

"You're asking me to marry you? For real?"

He stiffens and pulls back from me, and my heart stops beating for a few moments.

"You're right. I did this completely wrong." He gets down on one knee in front of me and fiddles with his hands, then looks at me.

Those stunning eyes, crowned by thick brows.

This prince is addictive.

He's royalty.

Everything I would ever want in a man.

And he's about to propose to me…

My eyes prick with tears while my heart clenches. This can't be right… can it? Is he pranking me?

"Guendolyn, will you marry me?" He stretches out his open palm toward me.

Shock hurtles through me. I adore this fae beyond belief… Hell, I love him.

Emotions tumble through me so fast I can't think, and I rush into his arms as he stands, tears running down my cheeks. We collide spectacularly, and he embraces me, lifts me off my feet.

"Oh, little wolf, you are so beautiful. And that's a yes then?"

I'm laughing, and when he finally puts me back onto my feet, I wipe my tears and nod crazily. "You're being serious, right? Like a real marriage, not a ruse just to get me to stay in the castle?"

Luther's face morphs into a serious look, and he cups my face, forcing me to look at him. "I do not joke about these things. My intentions are to marry you for life. I hadn't intended to ask you here and now, or like this, but I love spontaneity. It's been that way since you entered our lives." He kisses me as his thumbs wipe away my tears. "I love you, little wolf."

My whole body trembles to hear those words. I keep my eyes trained on his, at the way he smiles at me with genuine emotion. There's no teasing or assessing, just a fae opening himself up to me.

He lifts my hand, and I look down as he pushes a ring on my finger. A dark metal intertwined on itself like a vine. One line is studded with diamonds, the other filled with an electric blue stone that glimmers like a moving ocean. "This is beautiful."

My heart beats too fast with the emotions building inside me.

"This belonged to my grandmother, and she made me promise I gift it to my future wife. It's black gold with dragon tears and lava from the oldest volcano in our realm, the one they say the first fairies emerged from."

I glance up at him. "Wow, are you sure you want to part with it?"

"I've been carrying it around with me since we got back from Ash Court, trying to find the right time to give it to you. In fact, Deimos and I were meant to do this together, so I kind of stole that from him. Oops."

I run my finger over the surface of the ring that fits perfectly on my finger and throw my arms around Luther's neck, then shower his face with kisses.

"Yes," I assure him. "Yes, I want to marry you and Deimos. I wish he was with us too."

Luther kisses me firmly, his hands gripping my arms as I melt against him. Fingers slide over and cup my breasts, squeezing them. I moan against him as he pulls at the laced-up ties across my chest, loosening the bodice. Then he pushes the fabric down my shoulders and body until it falls into a heap around my feet.

Coldness creeps over my back from the window behind me, and I tuck myself against Luther. With my breasts against his bare chest, the heat is instant. My prince. My fiancé. My husband to be.

This is definitely going to take a lot of getting used to. Maybe for once, things are going to start going right for me.

"You are divine, and I'm going to devour you tonight." Luther steps back and eyes me head to toe, and the erection growing in his pants does not go unnoticed.

My whole body burns while I pull at his pants,

needing them off already. The moment I tug them open, his cock springs out like a jack-in-the-box, and I can't help but laugh. He's so huge, the long vein running down the front of his shaft thick, his tip coated in pre-cum.

Not wasting a second, he drops his pants to the floor and steps out of them, then takes me into his arms. Pressed together, I lean in and kiss him as he slides a hand down my leg and guides it around his hip, then does the same with the other. He walks me over to the wall away from the window and cages me in with his body.

"Tonight is just the beginning to all the ways I'll fuck your sweet, tight pussy."

Arousal claims me, consumes me. I want it to rip away everything else so nothing remains but the raw emotions we share. "I'll hold you to that," I answer and grasp onto his strong shoulders, drawing him closer and kissing him. The tip of his erection slides over my heat with the promise of so much more.

"Tell me what you want," he commands.

"God, I want you so badly." I shudder with need and arousal, my body scorching hot, my focus on where we're merging.

He's breathing heavily, teasing me. I shift to

better accommodate him—my prince is a very big boy.

"Say it," he demands, his hands to my throat, keeping me in place firmly but not painfully.

"Fuck me, please. I can't wait any longer."

He laughs and starts pushing into me, gradually at first, stretching me. My toes curl and I hiss out as my head falls back against the wall. He never relents, but moves all the way in, all the way to his balls.

He groans, sucking in air. "Fuck, you're so incredibly tight." Slow at first, he pulls out of me then moves back in, his pace picking up. Friction builds between us, igniting me.

Digging my fingers into his arms, I hold on as he thrusts into me, harder, faster now. His muscles tense and shift beneath my body.

"You will always be mine," he groans as he fucks me like nothing else in the world matters. His gaze never breaks from mine, and it reminds me how much I fell for him even before we met, how my heart beat for him even before I ever admitted it to myself. He watches me moan as I bounce up and down on his cock. "No one can even come close to what you mean to me. To how beautiful you are. To how perfect your sweet pussy is. Ever."

"I love when you say those things." My words are breathy, exhilaration building in me. He lets go of my throat, hands on my hips as he grinds into me. Seconds later he wrenches me toward him and walks us to the bed with him still embedded in me. Lying me on my back, he slides off, and I moan my protest.

"On your hands and knees," he orders.

"Oh yes, please." I roll over and prop myself up just as his hand gives my ass a hard slap. "Ouch." The word comes out involuntarily, but there's no denying there was something delicious about how good that felt.

He growls deeply, grabbing my hips and drawing me backward so my knees balance on the edge of the mattress, my ass high in the air and everything I have exposed.

"I love you looking this way." His cock pushes into my entrance, and in a heartbeat, he plunges deep.

I scream from the sudden explosion of pleasure.

"Fuck!" he snarls. "You feel so good." He hammers into me, the slapping sounds a gorgeous song of our love. His hands grasp my ass cheeks, kneading them, spreading them, then he curls a hand around my waist, finding my clit.

"I want to feel you coming with me buried in you."

Groaning, I fist the bedsheets as he spears me over and over. I slide toward the edge fast, my orgasm building with each passing moment, mounting as Luther takes me.

His finger strokes me to the point where I peak so fast that my climax comes at me suddenly. Tearing through me, my body convulses, and I cry out as I fall with the pleasure, my arms giving out as I collapse forward, my ass still high and Luther fucking me faster.

I scream out, orgasming long and ferociously, my whole body clenching.

Luther snarls like a beast, stiffening as he explodes inside me. "Squeeze me, that's it."

We both float on the clouds, attached and shuddering with the desire binding us. I no longer know where I begin and he ends. My heart thumps harder.

When we both come down from the most incredible orgasm, he slides out of me and we collapse on the bed. He draws me toward him, and

I roll into his arms, both of us sweating and gasping for breath.

He kisses my brow. "Are you ready for more?" he asks eagerly, and I'm not sure if he's serious, considering we're still both puffing.

"Absolutely," I respond regardless, and he shuffles out of bed.

It seems he was one hundred percent serious, and I'm blown away by his stamina.

"Spread yourself for me," he demands. "I'm going to clean you up first."

I roll onto my back and obey him, adoring the way he commands me in the bedroom. There's nothing more thrilling than a delicious man dominating you when it comes to sex.

He stands before me, his gaze dipping to the apex between my legs. A tingle of desire curls deep in my stomach, even though I've just climaxed.

"Don't move," he tells me. "We're not even close to being done."

My breath catches in my throat—I'm ready to go all night.

CHAPTER 10

GUENDOLYN

A coldness wraps around me, and I open my eyes to the sun beaming into the cabin through the gaps in the curtains. It takes mere seconds for my memories to return, and I lift my hand to stare at the ring on my finger. I still can't believe this is real. What we experienced was pure magic, and I want more.

I'm engaged to a prince. A fae prince, precisely, and butterflies whirl around in my stomach, twisting me into an anxious mess. While hundreds of questions and concerns pelt into me about how it all went down, I shove them away. *Not today, bad thoughts. I've ridden a terrible storm for too long, so give me this moment of joy. Everything else we can work out later.*

I mean, never in a million years did I ever think I'd find a prince, let alone marry one. So this is utterly surprising. It's the things fairy tales are made of and the best thing to have happened to me.

Rolling over onto my side, I reach out for Luther, except my hand falls through the air and lands on his empty side of the bed. I sit up and scan the cottage.

"Luther?" I call out in case he's in the bathroom, but when no response comes, I wrap the bedsheet around my naked body and pad across the cold wooden floor. The fire has burned out, so the air is crisp and cold.

When I knock on the bathroom door and there's no response, I open it.

He's not in there. Suddenly, his absence makes the cottage feel lonely and sad.

I frown and march over to the window. As I draw back the curtain, I see a guard standing outside with his back to me. The storm has passed... has Luther returned to the castle without me?

Why's there a guard outside? First, I need clothes. Quickly, I rush to get dressed, then I pat down my wild hair and open the front door.

Michae stands tall and greets me with a smile. "Morning, my lady."

"Where's Luther?" I groan.

"Prince Luther was called to an urgent matter with his brother at dawn. I am here to escort you back to court."

I glance back at our love shack, a place I will never forget as the place where Luther proposed. Sure, it was the strangest proposal, but it'll always stay with me.

"Are you ready to leave?" Michae asks.

I step outside and draw the door shut behind me. "Should I clean up the room, perhaps, before we leave?"

He smiles so genuinely at me, that I wonder if he must think me strange to ask such questions. "Maids will be arriving soon to clean everything. You don't have to worry."

I track behind him to a horse carriage waiting farther down the snowy path, reminding myself that having others clean up after me is something I will need to get used to. I'm pretty sure the guilt will vanish soon enough.

We ride under a stunning azure sky, no trace of the savage storm that roared all night. As did my prince. The thought brings an electric buzz racing up my spine. That fae has insane stamina. We went all night and only fell asleep in the early hours of the morning.

Once back at the castle, I head down to the baths for a wash, after which I dress in a brand-new, simple straight gown the color of my ruby. This time I include underwear that look more like white shorts.

Once I spot Michae go down the hall for a break from watching my door, I sneak out, hurrying down the corridor of the mansion. I have to speak to Deimos, but I can't have Michae following me and hearing my conversation with him.

I keep admiring my ring, at the way the dragon tears, as Luther called them, sparkle in the light. Part of me feels guilty that Deimos wasn't with us, that he may not agree to Luther having done this on his own. The last thing I want is to create any tension between the brothers, so I need to talk to him urgently. I think of what Ahren's reaction would be, but I don't even know what to make of that situation.

As I approach his room, a maid walks out carrying a bundle of bedclothes and dumps it on the wheeled trolley in the hallway.

On my approach, she lifts her gaze. "Miss." She gives me a small bow.

"Is Deimos here?" I ask.

She shakes her head. "He went up on the roof."

I frown. "How do I get there?"

She wipes her hands down her white apron, then glances over her shoulder down the corridor as if she's expecting someone to reprimand her for her talking to me. "Quickly, I will show you."

"Thank you." I take quick steps to keep up with her as she races down several hallways, then pushes open a door to a set of stairs.

"Go all the way to the top."

The stone walls of the circular enclosure are a dark gray, with narrow slits for windows. My skin pricks with the cold in here.

"Um, what is on the roof, exactly?" I turn back only to discover she's already marching back to the prince's room. If Deimos is up there, likely so is Luther, and even Ahren. As much as my stomach protests at seeing them all together, maybe it's not a bad idea to get everything in the open. To speak the truth about my engagement, about what is up Ahren's ass lately, and for me to tell them the truth of who my father was.

No more secrets. Tightness coils in my chest

about such a conversation, but if I intend to marry the princes and join their family, we need to come clean on everything.

I want us to start fresh.

Taking a deep breath, I step forward and make my way upstairs. It's quiet—there's no one else in here. It's only when I look out a window do I see how far up I am. I must be in a tower at the corner of the mansion.

Losing track of how many turns I've taken, I finally reach the top, my thighs smarting. Gasping for air, I pause for a moment to catch my breath so I won't appear flustered.

One last look at my ring, and I push the wooden door open. *I can do this.*

Bright daylight greets me, along with a faint breeze. I step out of the stairwell and onto an outdoor terrace. The mansion sits like a U-shape around the open balcony, which is enclosed by a stone railing. A table and several chairs sit in one corner, filled with platters of food and what appear to be paper scrolls. And there's only one lone figure up here.

Ahren stands at the other end of the balcony, hands on the railing, head low and staring at the kingdom grounds below.

Suddenly, I'm doubting my decision to be here.

"Lingering in the doorway is asking for trouble," Ahren states without looking my way, his voice deep and velvety. Just hearing him brings to the surface so many emotions—the pain of his rejection and secrets, how much I miss him.

I guess that is the best invitation I'll get from him, so I shut the door behind me and go to tuck my hands into pockets, except my dress has none. I've been keeping my ruby on the underside of my laced-up corset where there are layers of fabric. It's amazing what perfect little pockets they make.

Fidgeting, I chew on my lower lip and saunter toward him while my stomach does somersaults.

"How much trouble are we talking about, exactly?" I murmur upon approaching him.

"The kind that seems to follow you around." There's a tenderness in his voice; the words aren't bitter or aggressive. They belong to the fae who made me fall for him.

Maybe this is my chance to finally speak to him, to find out what's going on. I move to stand alongside him and stare out over the town sprawled over the rising landscape. The cottages shine black beneath the morning sun with trims of varied colors around the roofs and windows. In the valley lies a river that seems to divide the town in two, and I try hard to imagine what it would have been like growing up here. But in all honesty, I can't even fathom that lifestyle.

My chance to grow up amid my kind was taken from me by an evil woman in Ash Court, and one day I'll find out why.

"Deimos and Luther should be back later today," Ahren explains without looking my way.

"Where are they?"

"On an errand outside the castle walls to escort visitors past the Bloodcursed."

My stomach clenches at the sound of them facing danger. "Why did *they* go out there instead of soldiers?" I sound protective of them, and dammit, I am.

"Our mother insisted they be the ones to meet with our father first."

I almost choke on my breath. "Your dad, the asshole who left your mother for another woman?" Not to mention the bastard who beat Ahren senseless growing up, ripped his wings until there was only bone left, and left the scars on his back that will be imprinted on my mind for eternity. "Why would you welcome *him* to your court?"

"It's not mine yet, and Mother accepted him for

the sake of kingdom alliances. We must all stand together against the Unseelie." This time, the bitterness surges through his voice.

"It's still wrong," I answer.

He glances over to me, the corner on one side of his mouth curling upward, those pale green eyes smiling while the wind catches his long white hair and pushes it off his face.

I lose myself in those few moments in his presence. He's spectacular. Handsome. Rugged. Dominant. Scary. And someone that makes my heart thud in my chest with need.

As much as my hands tingle to reach over to him, I fear I'd be pushing my luck, so I turn back to the view, my hands gripping the cold stone railing instead.

"I admire that you always speak your mind. That's one of the things that I hate about my role. Being unable to do so."

When I glance over to him, I notice him looking down at my hand, at the ring Luther gave me. Luther said it was his grandmother's, so Ahren would know exactly what it means.

A paralyzing dread crashes through me. It shouldn't, but I see how quickly Ahren's demeanor stiffens, jealousy curling behind his narrowing eyes. His breaths quicken, and I lower my hand by my side, feeling like somehow I've cheated on him.

"Ahren, it's not—"

"I'm happy for you. This is exactly what I wanted for you." His words are sour and dark.

I cringe on the inside.

His shoulders bunch up, and the corded muscles in his neck flex.

"You're happy that your brother asked me to be his betrothed?" I hate asking that question, but I refuse to believe he's happy.

"Of course." His voice deepens, yet he refuses to look at me.

My knees weaken. "And it doesn't bother you in the slightest?"

"Should it?" He shrugs.

I study his face, searching for the expression that tells me he's lying, but he's a blank page, so good at hiding his feelings. I'm dying on the inside. I'm no fool; I can tell he's pretending, but it still damn hurts to hear those words from him.

He doesn't even give me a chance to respond before he turns and storms away from me.

What the hell?

I'm moving before I make the decision and grab his hand, forcing him to stop and look at me.

There's a buzz that zips up my arm from our touch, and he flinches too, feeling the connection.

"Can you just talk to me, please," I plead.

He pauses and twists toward me, raising an eyebrow. "What do you want from me? To say that it rips me apart to see Luther's ring on your finger? That I want to shove my fist through a wall over and over until I feel nothing but excruciating pain?"

My head spins, and I tighten my hold of his hand. "Then why are you pushing me away?"

He lowers his gaze. "I need to leave. I'm not doing this."

"No," I challenge him, stiffening. "Just fucking talk to me." I'll lose my shit before I let him walk away.

He groans, making a sudden, painful sound as his back unexpectedly twitches while he rolls his shoulders.

"Are you hurt?" I scan his back, which is silly, as he's wearing a black tunic and I can't see through it.

"It's nothing. Look Guendolyn, I'm sorry if you think we had something, but we can't have a future together." His voice is so monotone and robotic, as though he's been practicing this line.

My fingers curl around his when he flinches once more, his face scrunching up as if he's drowning in agony.

"What's going on?" I ask.

"It's stress. I hold it in my shoulders. It's nothing."

My insides are sizzling with confusion, and I don't know what to say or do. Ahren is in obvious pain. Sure, he has too much going on, and it's getting to him. But is that all it is?

"You expect me to sit back and watch you fall apart? Let's go sit down and I'll rub your shoulders. It always helps me."

He tugs his hand free from mine, his face morphing into one of frustration and anger. "How much clearer can I be?" he barks. "I assumed you would have found out by now about me from one of the castle staff."

My back flinches as I straighten. "Find out what? The reason you supposedly want to move on?"

He's heaving, the struggle obvious in his eyes and the way his shoulders hunch, his body curving forward.

"Just tell me. Whatever it is, I'll understand," I persist.

He looks away, darkness swallowing his expression.

I should be mad at him.

Should be furious and storm away.

But I can't get my legs to move when the desperation to uncover the truth pummels through me. I need to know what is going on with him.

"Tomorrow…" he begins, but instead of continuing, he groans and drops to his knees, his back suddenly arching.

My stomach curls in on itself. "Ahren." I reach for him as he slumps forward on bent legs like he might be sick, and in a heartbeat, the sound of fabric tearing has me startling upright. He hisses through his teeth.

Only when I step back do I notice the shirt on his back is shredded and his wings are pushing out for release.

Like last time I saw them, they are mainly bone. And they're stretching outward on either side of him for escape, wrapping around him. My heart cleaves in half to see them this way, to know his monster of a father ripped the flesh off his wings— and yet, he's being welcomed into the kingdom.

I want to scream at the injustice and destroy the sonofabitch for doing this to his son.

Reaching over, I tenderly touch a wing.

He flinches from my touch. "I told you before, I'm broken," he snarls. "How the fuck am I meant to rule a kingdom when I can't even control my own body?"

His voice cracks, and my heart squeezes as though a hand has it in a death grip. All I want is to take away his pain.

That's when I realize that I don't completely have control of my body either, because I'm still by his side after he's repeatedly tried to push me away. But maybe my mind knows something I don't... there is something much deeper going on with Ahren.

My hand traces over the length of the bone in his wing, and I close my eyes, imagining the energy in my body going into his, healing him.

There's no guarantee this will work, but I can't sit back and watch him fall apart. It kills me to see him so broken.

Heat radiates from my chest, right where the ruby sits, so I turn my focus to that. My skin pricks in an instant as power flares over me, lifting every hair on my body.

Ahren roars. "What are you doing to me?"

I flip open my eyes as he rips away from me

and climbs to his feet, skeletal wings jutting outward. The shadow of his wings looms over me, making him appear so much larger than usual. It reminds me just how small I am in comparison.

He stumbles about when the first spark of electricity snaps across the bones of his wings. It flares like lightning, dancing across his back.

I hate hearing the agony in his voice, and I don't know what to do. Have I made a mistake by using my stone to heal him? What have I done?

At his side, I wrack my brain on how to fix this, how to eliminate his pain, but I come up empty. None of this is normal.

He roars, his back arching, white sparks popping across his back.

"I'm sorry," I murmur, placing my hands on him, but he pushes me away and I stumble.

Everything I try fails.

Ahren's legs give out and he's back on his knees, hands reaching up over his shoulders to try to reach his wings. I tell myself I tried to help him, but seeing him this way kills me.

"Ahren," I call to him when he curls in on himself, trembling.

Inside, I'm bleeding with guilt, and again I step closer to do something… anything.

Something blue catches my attention at the base of a wing, and I squint to get a better look. In a flash, a sudden wave of violet, turquoise, and pearlescent white rush over the bony limbs.

That's all it takes… a breath, a heartbeat, as a layer of membrane materializes before my eyes, knitting itself over his bones. The colors blend and swirl in playful waves as they weave the fabric of his wings.

My breath catches in my throat, and the sight of him completely healed fills me with a sense of serenity, satisfaction, and fulfillment. They still remain curled around him, like a thin layer of colored stretchy fabric, and I can't stop staring at how spectacular they are.

"Oh. My. God! Ahren." I crouch in front of him, nudging him in the shoulder. "Get up."

He lifts his head to meet my gaze, his face pale, lips tight.

"Your wings," I whisper. "They're beautiful."

He blinks with confusion, then twists his head around to take them in. There's no response at first; he's just silent, frozen in time like the shock of healing is too much for him to bear.

He stands up in all his glory, the colors on either side of him like stained glass. They're captivating and brilliant, like the first blossoming buds in spring. They stretch out, spanning most of the balcony length.

His hand reaches out as a wing curls around to meet his touch. He swallows loudly, his mouth parted, and when he looks at me, his eyes glint with fresh tears. With the agony of seeing something I am sure he'd resigned himself to never experiencing ever again.

"How…" His shaky words trail off, and he grabs me by my arm and hugs me tightly. His heart beats ferociously in his chest, breaths racing, and tears prick in my eyes at his reaction. All I've ever wanted for him is to love himself despite what his asshole of a father did to him. This is the least I can give him.

I wrap my arms around his waist as warmth floods me at having him back. I don't understand how I can be so attracted to three men at once, but I don't care about that anymore. Right now it's just us, isn't it?

His grasp tightens, and my feet suddenly lift off the terrace. My heart thunders. I glance up at Ahren as he stares down at me, smiling like nothing in the world can touch him. The world falls away below us as his wings beat, air buffeting into us, hair fluttering around us, but I never break our stare.

"This is incredible," I gasp.

"I don't know how you managed it, but you've given me something I can never repay you for. You can't even begin to understand what this means to me." His voice cracks, and the sight of his joy loosens at the corners of my eyes.

"I want you to feel whole and not be reminded of what your asshole father did to you. There's—"

He leans and steals my words with a searing kiss, so powerful, so possessive, that it leaves me trembling. This is the Ahren I've missed, the fae who captivated me. I reach up and cup his face, pushing myself closer, kissing him back, showing him how much he means to me.

My heart almost explodes from the sheer happiness of being in his arms. Our kiss is fire; this is how we should always be. His tongue swirls over my lips teasingly while my stomach flutters with exhilaration.

"I've wanted you from the first time you arrived at our court, which was a mistake on my part. You deserve everything and so much more." A flare of uncertainty brushes over his face, and we're floating back down to the balcony.

Unease rises through my stomach, and the truth pushes to the forefront of my mind.

He doesn't intend to be with me, after all.

No, he wouldn't do that. Because the way he just kissed me belongs to a fae who is desperately in love.

My feet softly land on the floor, first my toes, then my heels. Ahren doesn't let me go and says, "I want your happiness." He pauses, and my heart stops for a moment.

"And?" Tears already blur my eyes because my body knows what's coming. I feel it twisting inside me, the agony squeezing, squeezing, squeezing until I can barely take a breath.

"I am to marry the princess of Ember Court in order to claim the throne of Shadow Court."

The sucker punch comes fast and instant, and I can't think at first. Tears fall; there's no stopping them. This is why he's been pushing me away, why he's doing it again now.

I stumble backward from him, utterly broken. This can't be right. It's me he is supposed to be with... how dare he marry someone else!

"Guendolyn, please. I have no choice in this." He reaches out for me, but I push his hand away.

The world freezes around us. There's nothing left.

I'm shaking my head, wiping my eyes, and my mind is spiraling. "I thought…"

How could I have been so blind to not see this coming? Of course he'd have to marry—I should have seen this. But in truth, it never once occurred to me that I'd lose Ahren. In my mind, we were secure and the problem was related to something else. I'm such a fucking idiot!

"If things were different," he begins, but I can't do this. I can't be in his presence.

"Don't."

The heartache in his eyes when he looks at me buckles my knees. My gaze lingers on him a bit longer, tracing every bit of him—his sharp cheekbones, the fullness of his tempting lips, the strong line of his jaw. But the longer I look at him, the more my body is ready to collapse, but I refuse to cry desperately in front of him.

I turn and run across the balcony and through the door. I don't stop moving as I race down the stairs. Tears drench my cheeks while on the inside I feel pathetic.

Stupid.

Naïve.

Foolish.

My lips feel bruised from his rough kiss. It's a reminder of something we can never have again. Here I assumed we were making up, that I'd given him a gift of his wings and in exchange he'd take me back. But that was just me being desperate, wasn't it?

Our time together was nothing more than a farewell.

CHAPTER 11

GUENDOLYN

Shock rattles me, digging its claws into me as I rush down the stairs from the balcony. I want to vanish from this whole damn kingdom. Shoving the bottom door open, I burst into the hallway and swing toward my room to be away from everyone. Especially Ahren.

I hate him for making me feel like shit, for rejecting me. And what I loathe even more is that in the back of my mind, I partly understand why he's doing it. That doesn't help me in the slightest. I want to detest him and remove him from my thoughts and memories as if we'd never met.

I wipe my eyes as the tears keep flowing. His decision cleaves my heart in half. How could I not have seen this coming? I've made a fool of myself.

There's no way I can live here and see him with someone else every day.

Thinking about the marriage about it makes me feel sick.

I stumble forward, sobs wracking through me, and I bump into the wall where I cry in my hands. My chest burns at the thought of seeing another woman in his arms. He is meant to be mine… and he knows it. I felt it in his kiss.

How did this become such a fucking mess? Do I really belong here anyway? Luther proposed to me, and I haven't even spoken to Deimos about it yet. But now that earlier joy is stained by Ahren's news. I twirl the ring around my finger, not sure what I'm supposed to do.

After everything I've gone through with the princes, I fell in love with them. With each one of them.

Luther.

Deimos.

Ahren.

Except Ahren has broken my heart, and I'm not sure I can recover if I'm reminded daily of what I lost.

I pull out the ruby from the inside of my corset and roll it over my fingers. There's still so much about myself I haven't uncovered, and the plan wasn't for me to fall for three princes.

The more I stare at the stone, the more I contemplate using it to just vanish out of here and return home to Earth. Just to think things through, to feel normal and blend into society like a nobody. I never thought I'd actually crave such a thing. I keep thinking how most of my life was a lie, and that pattern seems to be following me here too. Ahren's secret has ruined me, and I'm not sure how to get over it.

One minute, I'm ecstatic; the next, I want to run away. I'm growing tired of the drama and danger at every turn.

Footfalls resonate behind me, and my stomach clenches as my thoughts fly to Ahren.

I turn to find someone right in my face, and it's not the prince.

"Jasion!" His name rolls off my tongue with a gasp.

I stumble backward, and his gaze falls to my hand as I curl my fingers around the ruby stone.

"What's in your hand?" he demands, towering over me, his mouth in a sneer.

The bastard hates me, and the feeling's mutual.

"Leave me alone." I pivot away from him, my skin crawling in his presence.

Strong fingers snatch my wrist, and he tugs me backward. "I asked you a question."

Everything is getting to be too much for me. I just want to collapse and cry, to try to process what happened with Ahren and not deal with this idiotic mage.

"It's nothing." I wrench my arm from him, but he's not letting me go.

His nostrils flare as he glares down at me like I'm nothing. Arrogant asshole.

"You stole the king's ruby." He spits the words, saliva splashing onto my face, and I cringe.

I wipe my face with the sleeve of my dress. "Gross, keep it in your mouth."

His grip squeezes harder, making me wince.

"I thought I saw you playing with a red stone the other day, and then when I checked the throne and found the ruby gone."

Ice fills my veins that he was able to catch me with the ruby. I've been too careless with it, and now I reprimand myself for not being smarter about hiding it.

"I asked a few questions, and it seems the ruby

went missing about a week before our king was brutally murdered."

A cold shiver runs down my spine at his accusation, but there's no way I'm telling a mage of all people that a fairy took the stone.

"Give it to me!" he growls, leaning in closer.

The hatred in his voice triggers something in me. I've had enough of everyone. I'm trembling with anger.

"Fuck you!"

He snatches my jaw hard, hurting me even more after his last attack, drawing me to his face. That's when I see the shadows of guards coming up behind him. Are they escorting the princes? Except Ahren said Deimos and Luther were out of the kingdom.

"You murdered the king," Jasion hisses in my face.

Ice fills my veins at his words. "Are you crazy?" I shove a hand into his chest, but he doesn't move.

"The gem is priceless; you killed him to take it. What was your plan? Sell it and make a small fortune, thinking we'd never find out? That's why you played the princes, isn't it?"

I clench my fists, sick and tired of his crap.

Fury flares across my chest, spreading through me like an inferno.

"I am not a killer. And if you want the damn thing, take it." I swing my arm to toss the stone aside, but my hand and ruby slap against the wall.

Crack.

Sharpness digs into my palm, and shards of the shattered ruby fall to the floor as I draw my hand back. Blood spills from the cuts and pieces embedded into my skin.

"Oh shit," I cry, the pain sudden and sharp, feeling like the world's worst paper cut.

"You whore." Jasion shoves me to the side, right into the arms of a guard.

My world spins. The guard's hand is like a shackle on my wrist, and I'm being dragged behind him before I can even respond.

"Let me go," I bellow, punching his arm with my free hand. But it's useless because he doesn't react. He's walking so fast, he's practically dragging me down the hall.

I scream, needing someone to hear me and call Ahren. But the place is empty. The guard shoves open a door, and I'm wrenched in there with him, then I'm stumbling downstairs.

My heart is pounding in my chest as fear

collects inside me. Behind me, footsteps race closer, and I look back to Jasion and another beefy guard built like a barrel.

"I did nothing wrong!" I yell at him over my shoulder. I'm so damn furious that he caught me off guard.

Jasion smirks, staring at me with ill intent.

Next thing I know, I'm shoved through another door, and I stumble into a dimly lit room that smells like socks and the horse stables.

"Where are you taking me?"

But none of them answer. The guard hauls me along the dark corridor, then down another set of steps, and only once we go through another door do I realize where we are.

Prison cells line one side of the room. Brick walls divide the four enclosures, all of them empty.

My stomach drops through my body while panic strangles me. Despite my hand stinging and bleeding, I shove my elbow into the guard's gut, but he doesn't react.

"The princes will have your head for doing this," I threaten as I'm pushed into the open cell. A snap of energy strikes like a severe electric shock the moment I stumble over the threshold. I shudder and coil back around to escape.

"That's where you belong, assassin." He shuts the barred door with a deafening bang.

I rush forward and grasp a metal bar with one hand, shaking it. I don't feel the pain in my hand; I can only focus on the terrifying reality of what's to become of me.

"Let me the fuck out of here. I didn't kill anyone." My voice echoes around us.

Jasion steps in front of the door, hands folded over his bare chest, looking smug and proud of himself.

The hairs on my arms rise as a trickle of energy dances under my skin. The same kind I experienced back in Ash Court when I fought for my life.

"Let me out before the princes make you pay severely for this."

He chuckles to himself. "You actually think they'll find you? You'll be long gone before that happens."

Anger skyrockets through me. I grind my teeth as I call to the power as I had once before, but nothing happens... it doesn't respond. I fist my hands, my shoulders curling forward, and death plays on my mind... the death of this fucking sonofabitch.

The hatred in his eyes would kill me if they could form daggers. He's a piece of scum.

"You stand in my way, and that's the problem. But not for much longer."

The prick steps forward, just out of arm's reach, his head cocked to the side. The smugness on his face is infuriating. He tsks and sighs heavily like I'm a nuisance to him. Asshole.

"I'm doing you a favor. Do you know what they do to assassins here? Not even your princes will be able to save you from a brutal, long, and painful death."

"You've got it backward. I'm going to enjoy seeing the princes slice you apart with their swords."

"Maybe I'll change my mind and feed you to the wolves sooner than I thought. I have pieces of the ruby stone." He taps his pocket. "All the evidence I need to convict you. Along with a few witnesses. The princes won't be able to save you."

He whips away from me and storms down the long corridor, the guards on his heels. Seconds later, a door slams shut, and I'm alone.

Fear chokes me as I stumble back, hugging myself. A torch sitting in a metal bracket on the wall outside my cell is all that lights this place. A putrid, filthy, sorrowful dungeon.

I pace back and forth, screaming for help.

But will anyone hear me? We came down so many flights of steps, and... and I'm going to die here! I fucking hate Jasion, and when I get the chance, I will kill him with my own hands.

I stand in the cell, sick to my stomach wondering how the hell this happened.

When I look down at my bleeding hand, I become even more furious. I can't believe that on top of everything, I also managed to smash the ruby, meaning if I open a portal, I could end up anywhere. I want to cry, but I'm too numb. Instead I return to the cell door and scream for help.

DEIMOS

"Fuck, Luther, I thought we were doing it together?" Some days I want to punch my brother so hard for the simple satisfaction of how much he frustrates the hell out of me.

"The moment felt right." He shrugs and stares out at the snow-covered woodland surrounding us.

Guards are behind us. We left the kingdom

with help from the mages, making us undetectable by the Bloodcursed for just long enough to race away from the castle where they linger.

"We were alone," Luther continues, justifying himself. "Stuck in the cottage out in the woods during a storm. And well, the discussion came up, and it just happened that I had grandmother's ring on me."

I narrow my gaze at him with pure disbelief. "You've carried that thing with you since you were eight when she gave it to you, so don't fucking lie to me."

He glances over to me from atop his black mare, half smiling, not remorseful at all about asking Guendolyn to marry him without me there. "You really want to do this now, while we're going to meet Father?"

"Fuck yes," I say. "We had agreed, but keeping your word is impossible for you."

"What are you angry about the most, brother?" he snaps back. "That somehow you think you'll miss out, or that I spent a night with her and you didn't?"

"Fuck you." In truth, he's right on both accounts, but I won't admit it out loud. I'm still pissed at the stunt he pulled. I turn my attention to the landscape, keeping an eye out for Bloodcursed. That is the focus, not the fire brewing in the pit of my stomach that I wanted to be there for Guendolyn.

The more I think about it, the more sure I become that I want to hold my own proposal to her, with my own ring. It feels right that she has one from each of us. Once we arrive back, I'll put that into action. In all honesty, I wanted us to do this before she found out Ahren was marrying someone else. For her to know she wasn't alone, that she always had Luther and I.

It's not too late, but we have to escort our dickhead father back to our home. First get this worthless exercise out of the way, then I'll be back in the castle with her.

"I still don't understand why we have to greet the bastard," Luther growls in my direction as our horses trot alongside one another along the wide path.

The sunlight is bright, the sky clear, but being out here is the last thing I want.

"Mother insisted." If it was up to me, our real father would have never been invited to Ahren's wedding... and this is why I detest political bullshit.

Luther grumbles something under his breath,

his knuckles white from how tightly he holds the reins. We all hate our father for different reasons, but at the core of the problem, he's an arrogant turd who puts wealth and status before family.

"You think he'll bring his bride?" Luther sneers when he asks the question. The woman is young enough to be our sister.

"Might be awkward, but it wouldn't surprise me."

"I was thinking the same. It's another opportunity for him to rub it in Mother's face. Maybe we can speak to the chef about slipping something special in their meals so they spend the night in the toilet rather than at the ceremony."

"Get it done, and I won't tell a soul."

The evil smirk on his face has me grinning. Growing up under Father's thumb, the only way Luther and I survived was to make jokes, pull pranks—anything other than constantly fear his wrath.

We soon reach a crossroads. Straight ahead goes to Ash Court, and the other two lead toward the east and west kingdoms.

Standing before us are a dozen soldiers on horses, and near them is a golden carriage pulled by two mares. So he brought his bride after all. I sigh.

Our father rides forward on a large chestnut horse. He's filled out, grown stocky since we last saw him years ago. Gray streaks his short, dark hair, eyebrows bushy, and he's dressed in a thick winter coat the color of the blackest night.

"Luther, Deimos," he announces upon approach. Our guards part for him to join us.

Father pauses in front of us, permanently wearing that angry expression like he might strike out unexpectedly. Except we're not kids anymore. He is a lord, while we're princes, and hitting us comes with death, no matter who you are.

"So they sent you two? Not even His Highness can pull himself from his new throne to meet his old father." His nostrils flare, but I don't even speak to the man. The fact I'm out here is more than enough.

"Welcome." Luther sits tall on his horse, taking the high road. "The woods surrounding Shadow Court are dangerous. You will see Ahren and Mother soon enough." There's bitterness behind Luther's words.

Father snorts, his nose wrinkling. "Right, your land is still cursed. Shame, really."

With the vile smile tugging on his lips, it's easy to see he's enjoying every chance he gets to remind us of our downfall.

I grind my teeth, wondering if anyone will notice if we accidentally feed him to the Bloodcursed.

He glances over his shoulder and gives a low, short whistle at his men, and they begin coming toward us.

Father swings back to us. "Let's get moving. My ass and legs are aching from the saddle, and I want to hear everything about how King Tibout died. I've been hearing some strange rumors about your court, like a breach of Bloodcursed and fairies. Boys, maybe my arrival is exactly what Shadow Court needs."

He rides up ahead of us as though suddenly he is in charge. My insides sear with fury, and when I glance over to Luther, the corded muscles in his neck twitch.

Gods, it may not be the Bloodcursed that kills our father after all.

"Get the fuck out of my room, all of you!" I bellow, fury tightening my chest.

The council members abruptly stop their bickering and jolt to their feet. They look at me like they heard wrong, except I couldn't be more serious.

"Out!" I snap and whip around toward the balcony of my study... the king's study.

I don't have the patience today for their ludicrous ramblings about where different guests are to be seated at the wedding, the whole discussion on how the king will be buried after the wedding, and how I am to be relocated in the palace in preparation for my new wife.

The notion has me feeling trapped, and I'm

teetering on the edge of just walking away from everything. Everything I do is for duty, for loyalty, for my family.

But the cost is severe, and it's taking its toll on me.

All I can think about is Guendolyn and our time on the balcony. She healed my wings, eliminated the shadow I've lived under most of my life. And to thank her, I drove her away.

I'm fuming while my heart sits broken, a useless thing in my chest. How am I meant to marry another when the one person I would kill for is just out of reach? The hurt on her face is the worst... it destroys me to see her torn, to know I did that to her.

I clasp the railing out on the balcony and look down at the yard where guards and staff run around with decorations, making sure everything is perfect for something I don't fucking want. I'd give anything to be in their shoes, to just do a job and not have to make every damn decision for everyone. To be with who I want.

Tense, I grind my teeth, hating my life. I loathe getting up out of bed most mornings, and my stomach hurts unbearably. I can't remember the last time I had a full meal—nothing stays down anymore. I'm falling apart.

The door bangs shut behind me, and I twist around, expecting to find an empty room. Except Jasion remains, sauntering over to join me on the balcony, the fairy skull swinging from his neck annoying the hell out of me. It reminds me of Guendolyn. Everything does.

"Why are you still here?" I mutter.

"You're distressed. Good idea to get rid of the lot of them. They're a gaggle of geese going round in circles with no clear direction of what they want."

I return my attention to the grounds below. "And what do you want?"

He sucks in a sharp breath. "For Your Highness to be happy, of course. Remember all those years you spoke about what sort of king you'd become when it was your turn? How you'd make the kingdom a better place, ensure fairness and equality of wealth? I worry you've lost that spirit. Maybe the reality of being king is a lot more stressful than any of us realized."

His voice grates on my nerves, his words like a mosquito, constantly in my ear.

I straighten and face the mage as he leans over

the balcony railing to stare at everyone working tirelessly in the courtyard. "Don't give me your pity, Jasion. What do you really want? I can tell when you're leading up to something."

He coils around to meet my gaze and squares his shoulders. His hair is wild today—more than usual—peppered with tiny feathers, which means he's been practicing magic.

"I worry for you," he states, like he does all the time.

But my thoughts sweep back to my discussion with Luther on our way to Ash Court, where he insisted Jasion was infatuated with me. I've heard similar rumors for years, but I never paid them any attention. Jealousy comes in all forms—except when I study the way he looks at me, it makes me wonder.

"What you need is a close advisor by your side who isn't a dusty old rat who'll leak information to anyone for gold coins."

I frown at him. "What are you implying? That my royal council isn't to be trusted?"

He breathes heavily like he carries the world on his shoulders. "Ahren." He steps closer—too fucking close for my liking. "Where do you think I learned that your wings are healed?"

I stiffen, his confession taking me aback. "What the fuck?" I growl.

His shoulders rise and stiffen. "You're missing the point. I am the only person on the council you can trust to have your back, so appoint me as your chief advisor to take some of the load from you. Let me deal with the intricacies of planning your wedding, of the funeral, of our guests. You should not be bothered by these things."

He has a valid point, but my attention remains on someone having watched me on the balcony with Guendolyn. Had they seen her healing my wings?

"What did they see?"

Jasion rubs a hand over his mouth as if having to think this through. "You were seen from the grounds elevating over the balcony, your wings bright and spectacular. This is a new start, like you were reborn, meaning you leave the past as just that."

I almost choke on the words 'new start.' What waits for me feels more like being herded into a corral where I'll be closed away for life.

"Leave," I command. "I need time to think."

"Of course." He bows his head and begins retreating. "Just remember, you don't have to do everything on your own. We've been friends for a long time, and I'm here for you."

His over-affection is wearing thin on me. While he makes some good points, I don't know how much faith I can put in him until I better understand his motivation. He and I may have grown up together in Shadow Court and shared experiences, but that also made me privy to the type of fae he is: manipulative, starved for attention, and in desperate need to prove himself. Those traits don't make him deadly. Yet with Guendolyn's mistrust of him and the conversations I've had with the king and my brothers about him cause me to question things. To look at him in a different light, which now leaves me now doubting Jasion.

Once he leaves the room, I turn back to look outside, needing to find a way out of my damn messed up life.

Guendolyn

*A*n ear-piercing screech rips me from my sleep—if you call slumped against the wall, hugging your knees on the filthy floor of a prison any kind of sleep, that is. I don't even know how much time has passed. A full night? Hours?

Footfalls sound, and I make out the sounds of two people entering the dungeon. My stomach growls, and I'm certain it's starting to eat itself. Aside from water, the guards haven't given me a morsel to eat. And that's if they come to visit me at all. I'm alone down here, leaving me nothing to do but stew on my hate for Jasion. I hate him with every fiber of my being. My throat is raw from screaming, but no one can hear me down here.

The bastard mage is going to get rid of me without anyone knowing what happened. The princes will think I vanished, or maybe used a portal to run away after discovering Ahren was getting married. But I'd never run from Deimos and Luther. My time here has given me perspective. Ahren pushed me away, and it's my choice what I do with that. Not him or anyone else. So once all this bullshit marriage business is over, I'm going to ask Luther and Deimos to move with me out of the mansion, maybe even the kingdom. I don't care where we live, but I can't be under the same roof as Ahren knowing he is fucking someone else. It will rip me to shreds more than it already has.

The murmur of voices hums in the air, but I can't quite make them out, so I push myself up to my feet and quietly tread toward the barred door. I look out, but from my angle, I can't see who it is beyond the brick walls of my prison.

"You did a good job," a bristly, dark voice says in a whisper. I don't recognize who it belongs to.

"Just as you said, the bigger they are, the faster they fall," Jasion responds, and my hackles flare. I clench my teeth when I hear him.

"And Ahren?" the man asks, his voice vicious.

I freeze in place.

"He'll slowly come around," Jasion explains. "Then once you relocate here, he's ours to sway."

I don't dare move, going over and over what I've just heard.

"Come, let me show you the girl."

My heart slams into my throat as their footsteps close in. I throw myself to the nearest wall and slump down onto my ass, head low as though I'm sleeping.

A loud whack of metal against the bars has me

jerking and snapping my eyes open. My breath catches as these two murderous monsters stare at me. Jasion and an older man with graying hair, wearing a long winter coat.

The older fae with longer ears leans forward, squinting his eyes to look at me. "So this is the whore who captured Ahren's attention? She doesn't look that special."

I hug my knees tight, unable to find any words that will make a difference to these two.

He tilts his head, studying me. I already detest this man as much as I do Jasion. I don't have a damn clue who he is, but I have to warn Ahren that he's in danger.

"She was found with the ruby from the king's throne. And she will be executed for treason before the whole kingdom the day after the wedding. But there's something special about her I haven't worked out yet."

The man sneers. "Get over here!" he barks at me.

I don't move.

Jasion glares at me. "Do as he says or I'll come in there and force you."

My skin crawls, and I want to scream at these

assholes to leave me alone. But I push myself to my feet nonetheless and move toward them.

"Hand," he demands.

I swallow hard, terrified. "Please don't hurt me."

"Give me your hand!" he shouts, and I flinch.

Considering my palm still hurts from my failed attempts to remove the shards of ruby, I stick forward my other arm.

He lashes out and snatches my wrist, dragging my whole arm through the bars. The side of my face slaps against the metal bar, my body shaking.

The bastard sniffs my hand, the sight sickening me.

I'm locked in place, my stomach tight. The man's expression gives little emotion. I get the feeling that maybe he's incapable of showing any feelings.

Jasion is in my face in seconds, smirking like a gutless asshole. "Not so tough now without your prince." He enjoys seeing me squirm.

As I suck in a rapid breath, I take in the scent of strong cloves... a familiar smell I can't place at first.

Then a sharp pain digs into my wrist, tearing skin, feeling like blades.

I scream and wrench my hand back to find a goddamn bite-mark. The old bastard drew blood.

"You fucking pig," I spit as I pull down the sleeve of my dress to cover the bite mark, pressing the fabric against the wound to soak up the blood.

The dickhead licks the blood from his teeth, his eyes fluttering upward for a moment. "You're right, she's more than just a healer. The magic sparks in her blood. She will destroy everything we have worked toward for years. Kill her!"

"No!" I cry out and recoil, my knees buckling. It's only by a miracle that I'm still standing.

"I'll arrange it shortly," Jasion answers, then looks my way with the threat clear in his eyes that he'd prefer to torture me than make it a swift ending.

The older sonofabitch groans and turns away. "I've had enough of this depressing dungeon. I'm starved."

"Of course, your lordship." They both stroll away, the man barking in laughter, until the clang of the main prison door shutting steals the hideous sound.

I can't move, not after everything I've just learned. Fear grips me, and dark whisperings of nightmares coming my way drag me under.

But like a spark, the scent of cloves I picked up on Jasion clings to my nostrils, and the reality of it slams into me like a wrecking ball. Michae said he found cloves near the king in the throne room right after he was murdered. I thought it had been strange at the time.

Fuck! Jasion used magic to murder the king. My father. I knew it.

My stomach drops right through me like a boulder.

And I'm next.

The asshole blamed me, using the ruby as evidence. I'm his scapegoat, aren't I?

My chest burns with rage, my heart beating so fast and hard, the room tilts around me. They killed the king in cold blood for Ahren to get into power, to use him as a puppet. But my prince isn't that stupid. He can't be.

I pace mindlessly in my cell, both hands now hurting terribly.

Anger surges like a tsunami through my chest, and nerves dance across my temple. Darkness begins to linger inside me. My time is coming if I don't get out of here and warn the princes.

All I can think about is them, my throat thick with terror that I won't get a chance to stop this.

I close my eyes and take deep breaths to still my raging heart, and a flare of power erupts down my arms. My power sparks as a sharp ache digs into my cut palm from the ruby. Is my ability fluctuating because I shattered the ruby?

There is only one thing to do and it's risk, but sitting here is not going to help me. I raise my hand covered in dried blood and bits of stone too small to remove, bringing it to my mouth and focusing on the image of a portal opening to my room in the castle. Then I blow out a breath.

A surge of energy rises through me and rolls out past my lips. A pale blue fog puffs out into the air, billowing all around the cell until it concentrates in a corner, darkening until all that stands before me is a black opening just large enough for me to enter. I don't wait a single second longer and lunge toward my escape.

As I step through the portal, I whisper, "Please don't let this be a mistake."

CHAPTER 13

I step out of the portal and emerge out into an oversized sitting room with pearlescent wallpaper. Long, narrow windows flood the room with natural light, while a fire roars from the hearth in the corner.

Ornate wooden furniture decorates the space, and carved display cabinets are packed with all manner of books and colorful gems. Only when I look over to the two couches facing each other do I notice the back of someone's head.

My heart beats frantically because nothing in this room looks familiar. I've seen enough of the princes' mansion to know they don't have windows like these.

I'd been trying to get the portal to take me to

my room, but obviously it didn't work. So where the hell am I?

I turn back toward the portal, except it's gone, and my insides freeze over.

Please, no! I raise my wounded hand, needing to get out of here fast. I give a quick blow over my palm, concentrating on my room in the mansion, yet not a single spark of energy comes. The more I try, the more I start trembling. This is the worst-case scenario, being taken to a random place. Sure, I escaped the dungeon, but where in the world did I land instead?

Wasting no time, I swing toward the black, wooden door and quickly grasp the handle…

"I wouldn't do that if I was you," a female's voice sweeps around me from behind.

My shoulder muscles bunch up, and I turn around swiftly.

Several feet away stands a jaw-droppingly beautiful woman who looks so familiar. She's older, maybe in her mid- to late forties, long blonde hair falling over her shoulders in soft curls. Delicate round face with the bluest eyes, pale lashes and deep red lips. She's slightly taller than me, curvy, and wearing a teal gown that's tight around her bust and billows outward like she has layers of fabric underneath. If there was ever an image of a perfect fairy tale princess, this woman was the epitome.

There's something quite familiar and calming about her.

"I-I think I've l-lost my way," I say softly, playing the innocent card.

She looks at me from head to toe, then to the door.

"You came exactly where you needed to," she answers. "The portal brought you here because this is your place."

What is she talking about? Looking around the room for anything familiar, I find nothing, and outside all that's in view are snow-covered woods for as far as the eye can see. There are no mountains, which is strange, as I'm used to seeing them from the mansion windows.

"Who are you?" I ask. "What is this place?"

She steps toward me, and there's a daintiness in the way she saunters. She is a woman of higher standing, someone used to always appearing perfect. I've seen the princes' mother, so I know it's not her.

But why is this woman locked in a room?

"Come with me." She offers me her hand, palm upward, the tips of her fingers slightly curled.

I should be afraid, but the energy around her calms me. There's something about this woman that makes me want to curl up and listen to her tell me tales. And she seems to know more about me than I do.

So I reach out and place my hand with the bite on my wrist in hers.

In response, she rewards me with a beaming smile that I feel deep inside me, like she's the sun filling me with a strange tranquillity.

She guides me over to a window, both of us standing side by side, staring outside to where the morning sun is just peering up over her horizon.

Down below is a lofty stone wall surrounding the building, the grounds dotted in trees, and beyond the barrier lies a creek frozen over by winter. Then the forest explodes outward in every direction.

It takes me seconds to realize I've seen this place before. I've been here... and as the memory hits me, I gasp and pull my hand from hers, wincing with discomfort from the bite.

The yard below is exactly where Deimos and I

first stepped out of a portal when he brought me to this realm.

I can't breathe.

I've teleported myself into Ash Court.

Fuck!

The woman smiles. "You remember, good. I watched you arrive that night from up here and have been keeping an eye on you ever since."

"How?" My knees wobble. The last time I came here, the king's mother tried to kill me, and well, will this woman do the same?

"There is so much I have to tell you. We don't have a lot of time—no one must find you here."

"Please tell me what's going on?" I hug myself.

She steps toward me, and I retreat.

"Let's take a seat." She waves for me to follow her back to the couch, where she sits and pats the seat beside her.

Not like I have many other options right now, and she hasn't threatened me, so I go and join her. She sits with her back straight, hands in her lap on the opposite end of the couch, facing me.

"I know who you are because I recognize the scent of your magic," she says. "I always knew you were powerful, with abilities like opening portals, like affecting other fae's abilities or vice versa. To me, you are beautiful, but your presence scares many others. You are a threat to them."

I wait quietly for more information, taking it all in, eager for the punchline to understand how all this ties together.

"What I was forced into doing to you has destroyed me." Her voice chokes. I don't even know this woman, but I lean closer and place a hand on her arm. She trembles under my touch.

"What do you mean?" I whisper, almost afraid to find out the truth.

She lifts my hand and kisses the back of my fingers tenderly. Not in a creepy way, but with a loving nature like I'd expect from a family member... a parent...

Then I see everything clearly, like a door has been opened in my mind.

The similarities I'm looking at are mine. The hair, the body shape, her tenderness. The agony that burns behind the gaze when she looks at me.

Tears prick my eyes. "Are you my mother?" My breath catches in my throat as her fingers tighten around mine.

"Leaving you in the care of the Women's Refuge on Earth was the hardest thing I've ever done, and I still haven't recovered." Tears slip freely down her cheeks. "You were just a baby, and if I didn't hide you, my husband and his mother would have killed you."

My head spins. I can't even respond at first from the shock of what I've just discovered. I try to hold myself strong, but my chin trembles. I shuffle closer, and she hugs me tight against her. I cry against her chest, and she's sniffling, both of us emotional wrecks. I always imagined laughing and smiling crazily when I finally met my parents, not crying.

But to discover I lost my father was devastating enough, and now... I found my mother. Is this why the portal brought me here when I asked for my room? It delivered me to where I belonged. To my mother.

Sorrow and unbelievable happiness twist inside me, tugging me in different directions until I don't know what I feel anymore.

I draw away from her and wipe my eyes with the back of my hand, then remember her last words. "I'm confused by so many things. You say my father wanted me dead, yet—"

"I didn't say *your* father, but my husband. I am married to the king of the Unseelie in Ash Court, but I never loved him. It was a forced marriage to unite two powerful houses."

"You're the queen of Ash Court!" I gasp and blink at her, processing everything I'm learning. "And you had an affair with the king of Shadow Court?"

Fresh tears gleam over her eyes at the mention of my real father, and she nods. "I loved him, but there was no way we could ever be together. Seelie and Unseelie don't mix."

I loathe that saying. I am a result of both, so I must be the most hated person in the world. I hold onto her arm and think how much it hurts to have Ahren taken from me, and I can see that same excruciating ache in my mother's eyes.

"Listen to me very carefully, Guendolyn." She leans in closer. "You are more powerful than any of us. The fairy blood that runs through my mother's family bloodline is the purest, from the queen of fairies herself. It's laid dormant in every generation since her demise, but when you were born, the fairies surrounded the castle in the hundreds of thousands, chanting the word *Eirian*."

"Fairy queen," I whisper.

"Yes, my little one. You carry the fairy queen's power inside your veins. It's one of the reasons the king and his mother wanted you dead. Your power is too great. It's why the king's mother put a curse on you when you were born, unbeknownst to me. She made it so that if you did somehow come back to our realm, your presence in our kingdom would unleash hell on the Shadow Court. A fitting punishment to King Tibout, my husband would remind me."

"So they knew you had an affair with the enemy king?"

She nods. "It's why I've been living under constant security for most of my life."

There's so much information coming at me that I sit back and try to sort through it all. Things are starting to make sense now... like the fairies' attraction to me, why everyone would hate me, and how I ended up on Earth.

"There's something else you need to know," she says.

"In all honesty, I don't know how much more I can take." With everything else that's happened in Shadow Court, all this news is overwhelming.

She continues regardless, "The main reason most fae want you dead is because you are the one true heir to reign over both Ash and Shadow Courts."

My mouth drops open.

She turns to me and grabs my arm tightly, her expression beyond serious. "King Tibout is gone. Before his son Ahren takes the throne, you need to claim that position and marry a royal quickly. Once you hold it, you will lay claim to the throne in Ash Court as well, meaning you can influence this court's decisions while the king and I still rule here. Once one of us passes, then you can claim this throne with your king and reign both courts. You will bring them back into one kingdom as it once was. The other kingdoms in the realms will join as well."

I'm shake my head. "What? You can't die!"

"Hush." She places a hand on my mouth. "I'm not going anywhere. I've waited for this moment for too long, I've lost too much—but now is the time to strike."

"I don't want the throne," I whisper.

"It's not about what you want, sweetie. This is the only way to stop the bloodshed between our courts, to end the deaths, to restore balance in our world."

I swallow past the mountain in my throat, pondering her words, mostly considering my three fae. "What will become of the princes? Can I marry one to take the throne?"

She looks at me strangely and smirks. "Has one caught your eye?"

I smile too widely, unsure how to tell her that it's in fact all three. "Sort of."

"To claim the throne, you must take someone royal as your king anyway, so yes."

There's an explosion in my stomach of anticipation and excitement at what she tells me. I can marry Ahren!

But just as fast, doubt settles in me as I consider the enormity of what she is proposing. "I'm not sure this is going to work. Why would they believe me when King Tibout can't back up my claim? And how does that unite the courts?" My knees are bouncing; I can't believe I'm even contemplating this. I barely understand fae customs, let alone know enough to rule. It's a joke to think that I could reign over anything when half the time I can't even control my own mouth.

"The answer is in your blood. Mages can test your bloodlines with magic—that is your evidence."

The mention of mages makes my skin crawl, because there is no way Jasion will ever help me.

But the king has other mages, so maybe I just need to get them on my side. My breaths are coming fast now, and I'm struggling to fill my lungs. Am I really thinking of trying to claim the throne?

I shouldn't feel guilty, though part of me wonders how Ahren will react to this. Me stepping in...

"Maybe this isn't the best thing to do. I just want to fit in somewhere and have a normal life."

My mother stares at me with sympathy and cups a hand over my cheek, rubbing my tears away. "The biggest mistake I made in my life was that I never fought for what I wanted. I let fear rule my decisions. As a result, I lost my daughter and the fae I loved. I don't want you to live with such regret. It eats away at you; it's crippling. This is your chance to take what you want, to make a difference in a world that once tried to kill you just because you were different." She gets to her feet and takes my hand. "It's time to stand and show everyone who you really are."

I don't move at first but look at her, and the question swirling on my mind comes forward. "Did my father know about me?"

Her head lowers, but I catch the glint in her eyes before she whispers, "Yes. But he lost the chance to meet you." Her soft, wavering voice breaks me. She moves across the room to a display cabinet and pulls a drawer open.

I'm on my feet and meet her as she turns around. Taking my good hand, she places a long, pink ribbon in my hand. The fabric is soft like silk under my fingers, and on one side my name is embroidered in white, repeatedly. *Guen.*

"Your father had this made especially for you and sent it to me, but you were already gone by then. I never told him it was too late; I couldn't." She covers my hand with hers, curling my fingers over the treasured ribbon. "I can now say I've kept my word to him." She hastily wipes a loose tear from the corner of her eye, and the ache in my chest intensifies.

Clearing my throat, I say, "I spent time with him in Shadow Court, but I don't think he knew it was me. He made me feel comfortable and welcome when we had the chance to speak."

She reaches over and collects my cut hand, still embedded with shards of ruby, and places it between her two palms. "Sometimes, fate has a way of uniting those who are meant to cross paths, even if they don't know it."

Suddenly, her touch sends a flare of scorching heat up my arm.

I wince, and she lets me go. When I look at my hand, the cuts are all gone, and only dried blood remains. I glance up at her, bewildered.

"I have the power of healing and a few other tricks."

So it's her I gained my healing from. When I look at my hand again, I can't help but wonder if she's sealed the shattered pieces of the ruby inside my skin.

"Call your portal," she says abruptly, her tone rushed. "There isn't time to waste."

"Wait, what about you?"

"The wedding is today," she whispers, "so stop the marriage and claim what is yours. I will be fine. You coming here has been promised to me by the fated fairies, and everything will change from now on. You will see very soon."

"There's already been so much change," I murmur.

"Quickly now, you must go and claim your true heritage. Nothing else matters."

I have so many more questions for her, but she's right. I need to stop Ahren from marrying someone else. I lift a shaky hand to my mouth and blow a breath, blue air misting outward past my lips. *Return me to the Shadow Court in—*

My words fade as the portal materializes before me within seconds. This has never gone so easily before. Is it the ruby inside me, or my mother's help?

"Go swiftly." She nudges me in the back.

I stumble forward and cross the threshold into darkness.

CHAPTER 14

DEIMOS

"Have you seen Guen...Gainy?" I ask the twentieth staff member this morning, almost slipping up her name each and every single time.

The maid shakes her head, her gaze low. "Sorry, Your Highness, but I've asked around too, and no one has seen her since yesterday."

I snap away from her and march down the hallway, then swing directly into her chamber again, but I don't even know what I'm searching for, what could possibly indicate where she's gone to.

Luther charges into the room behind me, and my heartbeat spikes with hope, with anticipation that he brings news.

But the devastation on his face sinks through

me, dragging me to a horrible place where I imagine that she's somewhere hurt. We never should have left her alone.

"Absolutely fucking nothing," Luther growls. "We've searched the palace and mansion, along with the grounds and town. I can't even reach her with my thoughts. Something's blocking her off from me."

I turn to my brother. "How did Ahren take it?"

Luther scoffs incredulously at my questions. "You think I'll tell him on his wedding day that the girl he loves has gone missing? But I did ask him when he saw her last, and like everyone else, it was yesterday."

I trudge over to the window, scanning the courtyard below for her long blonde hair, the adorable way she walks with a swing of her hips. I keep hoping I'll spot her and that this is just some huge misunderstanding. "He needs to know," I murmur as I turn to Luther. "Ahren will murder us if we don't tell him and she ends up hurt." I swallow against the lead ball pressing into my throat.

Luther runs his hand through his hair like he does whenever he's holding onto a secret. He's easy to read like that, plus his gaze is miles away.

"What aren't you telling me, brother?" I lean back against the couch, watching my brother, who stands several feet away by the window.

His head cocks up toward me. "Guendolyn healed Ahren's wings."

My eyes bulge. "That's incredible! He should be in a great mood then."

Luther's face scrunches up as his mouth tugs to the side. "Not quite. He told Guendolyn about his marriage and why he can't be with her. She ran away from him, and it's the last he's seen of her."

"Fuck, Luther, you could have started with that! So it means she's upset and maybe ran away to hide somewhere?"

Luther looks at me in disbelief like my suggestion is improbable. "She loves us," he says. "She wouldn't hide from us."

"We weren't here when she needed us most," I remind him.

His deadpan stare tells me everything. Yeah, we had no say in going to meet Father, but this fucking sucks.

"Alright," I state. "Where would someone devastated go?" Just saying those words out loud has my chest squeezing as I picture her somewhere alone and heartbroken. She needs to be in my arms where I can remind her she's *not* alone and explain why Ahren is in a shitty situation that will haunt him his entire life. I just wish Ahren would have spoken to her earlier as he promised he would.

I curl my hands into fists. This isn't how any of this is meant to play out. Luther and I had spoken about asking Guendolyn to marry us; we'd intended for the three of us to live in this mansion, making a new life together. It's everything I want, but I know she hurts for Ahren. And that's going to be a hard obstacle to overcome.

"We split up," Luther begins. "And we do another sweep, keeping in mind we are searching for places she'd use to escape everyone."

I nod. "We need to find her fast, as Mother will hunt us down herself if we miss the wedding. It's meant to begin shortly, and we're not even dressed yet."

Luther huffs. "I fucking hate this wedding." He pivots on his heels and storms out of the room and into the hallway. I do the same and decide to commence searching from the top of the mansion, then make my way down. There are so many empty rooms; maybe we missed something on the first sweep.

Around the next corner, I walk right into

Jasion, who rushes without looking. Stumbling back, I groan while he bows his head.

"Apologies, Your Highness, for not seeing you. This is a manic day, and I have so much to prepare for the ceremony."

As much as I dislike the mage, I don't miss the opportunity to ask, "Have you seen Gu-Gainy?"

He stiffens at my question, piquing my curiosity.

"Well?" I urge him, stepping closer, my gut twisting in on itself. I've always hated him. As far as I'm concerned, no one will miss him if he's booted out of our court.

"This morning," he says and clears his throat, lifting his gaze to me. "I saw her just after dawn."

Hope springs to life inside me. "Where?" I eagerly ask, leaning forward.

"I was looking out the window as I awoke, and she was running through the woods outside the kingdom walls."

"What?!" I shout, unsure if I heard right. "Are you sure you saw right? There are fucking Blood-cursed out there."

He nods, his face paling, and there's fear in his eyes. Fear of me—and this isn't the Jasion I know.

His behavior is strange, and that's saying a lot for him.

"I thought it was strange too, but I only saw her for a few moments and she was fine, so I just assumed all was well and someone was watching her back. I thought nothing more of it."

I'm fuming as I snatch him around the neck and slam him against the wall. "Why the fuck didn't you come and tell someone right away?"

He clasps my wrist as I squeeze his neck. How incredible it would be to get this weasel out of our lives for good. I've never liked or trusted him, but what reason would he have to lie about this? And… his story fits perfectly with the notion that she couldn't bear to be here during Ahren's marriage, so she ran away.

An invisible hand seems to wrap around my heart, constricting, the aching sorrow escalating. She wouldn't leave Luther and I… but that's something I struggle to believe, even after everything we've been through.

Jasion is hitting my arm, his face turning blue. Oh, right. Probably best I don't choke Ahren's mage to death on this auspicious day.

I pull my hand back and he falls to the ground, his knees buckling under him, gasping for air.

"The second you see her, bring her right to me, understand?" I growl.

He nods. "Of course, Your Highness," he croaks.

I can't stand to even look at him a moment longer, so I turn and march down the corridor, making my way down to the stables. Looks like I'm taking a quick trip along the walls for any signs of Guendolyn and pray to the gods that she's alive.

I'll tear down this whole fucking realm to find her if that's what it takes.

Guendolyn

I burst out of darkness and into a dimly lit room. My eyes scan the surroundings, expecting to see my bedroom in the mansion.

Except, that's not where I end up, is it? The stench of the dungeon assaults my nostrils as I stand right back in the locked cell.

"Oh, fuck no!" I spin toward the portal that has vanished and curse the damn thing for never listening to my instructions.

I rub my eyes from irritation, ready to scream. I

lift my hand to my mouth, but doubt floods me. God only knows where I'll end up. But when I remember my mother's words, I know I have no time to waste—I have to try.

Part of me just wants to celebrate that I found my real mother, that I finally understand my past. Sure, it was majorly fucked up, but it's a start to piece it all together and attempt to move on. So for that, I'll go in and out of my portal as many times as needed, pushing my limits until it takes me where I ask.

I remind myself that I have fairy powers, whatever that means. If I knew how to wield them, I'd zap out of here in a heartbeat and smite all those who've hurt me and those I love. Though considering how much difficulty I've had with utilizing my power, I somehow feel that it's going to take quite a bit of time to harness them.

Geez, what I wouldn't give for a manual— Using Fairy Powers 101.

A sudden creak of the main door into the dungeon erupts, along with footfalls.

I freeze over, terror clinging to me with the fear that it's Jasion returning.

Frantically, I press the base of my palm to my mouth, sucking in a breath.

"Gainy? What in the world are you doing here?" a familiar male's voice murmurs.

I twist my head and almost cry with happiness when I lay eyes on Michae. "Oh my god, you found me!" I dart across the filthy floor and lunge myself at the metal bars, shaking them. "Let me out, please, before Jasion returns."

"He put you in here?" His voice carries a quiver.

"The bastard accused me of killing the king and is planning to murder me, plus he's in cahoots with some old fae I've never seen before. God, Michae, please get me out." I'm rambling and bouncing on my toes, half expecting the mage to burst in here and murder him before he can set me free.

Michae searches the place but comes back with sorrowful eyes. "The spare key isn't here. I need to it."

I nod, my stomach twisting that he's going to leave me. "Please hurry!"

"Yes, I will," he assures as he rushes out, leaving me alone.

I pace back and forth and pray I'm not making the wrong decision to wait.

CHAPTER 15

AHREN

"Where are they?" I ask Mael, frustration bleeding into my tone. "My brothers couldn't have just disappeared."

His brown eyes are wild with worry, and he keeps combing his fingers through his short, white hair in a nervous twitch. Like everyone else, he's dressed for the wedding in black pants and a leather doublet with silver buttons down the front. The fabric pulls across his middle, and his brow is moist with perspiration.

"Your Highness, I've sent the guards for another search through the grounds. We will find them."

I huff and turn away, biting my tongue. It's not him I'm furious at. It's this whole fucked-up situation. I'm here, waiting for the maids to bring my ceremonial clothes, and it's killing me. I want this shit day over with.

Today I will marry a princess, a stranger, a woman I don't desire, and the coronation ceremony will take place immediately after. The kingdom is celebrating my ascension to king, and I tell myself over and over that once I am in that position of power, I can change things.

Well, all things except the ability to have the woman I want by my side.

I had hoped Luther and Deimos would join me today for support, but it seems I've been forgotten, left behind. One more reason to hate this day.

"Having cold feet?" a male voice slices through my thoughts, a voice that sends chills through me.

"Father," I hiss through clenched teeth and turn to find him walking into my chamber.

"I was rather disappointed, son, that it's only now I get a chance to come and give you my blessings. I always knew you'd rise to something big. You just needed the right push."

The corded muscles in my neck tense. "That's not how I remember it," I answer, exhausted of the games—and the day has only just commenced.

He smiles at me, a rarity from the man who

reminded me daily that I would never amount to anything, that I was weak, who told me that his beatings would strengthen me.

"Enough. Leave," I growl before I drive my fist into his face.

He doesn't move. "Son, I will admit some of the animosity between us might be my doing. I taught you the same way my father did me. Plus, I should have visited you here long ago to make peace between us. For that I hope you can forgive me, and we can begin a new path of truce."

I stare at him incredulously. Is he fucking joking? Who the hell is this man? My father would never grovel.

"What do you want?" I snarl, my pulse racing, throbbing through my veins.

The usual anger I'm used to seeing on his face is replaced with something pitiful. Has my father gone senile? Or did my mother invite him not just for the sake of diplomacy but because she has accepted the past as just that. Is this a clue that maybe we ought to do the same... if Mother can stand to face this fae for a few days to ensure relations with us and the east of the realm aren't broken, then maybe I can do the same?

"To be with my sons, and make up for lost time."

I struggle with my thoughts about following Mother's direction and blink at him in disbelief. Flames engulf my insides still the same. When I look at him, all I remember are his angry fits, the beatings, and the repeated times he ripped the flesh off my wings until it never grew back. That shit is something I'll never get over or forgive. I should have made it clear to my mother not to invite him.

"I don't have time for whatever scheme you have going, now that you know I'm about to take the throne. Maybe it's fear or stupidity that brings you here, but Father, the bridge between us fell apart long ago and there is no mending it."

He stares at me with contempt, an expression I'm much more familiar with. *There's* my real father. "I hope, over time, you can reconsider."

Without waiting, he lifts his chin high and turns around, his coat whipping around him as he leaves my room.

Today is going to kill me. It pisses me off that Mother insisted we invite that asshole to my wedding and coronation. It's a day I'll never forget, everyone tells me. And I agree, except it won't be for the reasons they assume.

Moments later, several maids appear at my door, looking at me expectantly. The brunette curtsies as she announces, "Your Highness, we are here to finish dressing you."

I huff. I know fighting this is futile. Such events are planned down to the most minute detail, so I wave them in, then let them fuss about with my clothes. I'm already wearing my black pants, and I remove my top to make it easier for the maids, who now flutter around me like fairies.

The thought of fairies brings Guendolyn to mind, and my heart constricts. Neither of us asked for this ending.

When the maids are finished, I look down at my deep blue, cut-velvet coat that drapes down to the floor. The edgings of the front and high collar are richly embroidered in gold, the designs resembling the sun and stars, the river and earth. The elements that combine to make up our realm. A maid takes my hand and pushes golden rings on my fingers, as is customary. Only one finger remains bare, waiting for the bride to adorn it during the ring exchange.

The ladies step back and admire me. They

smile, proud of their work, but I feel like a fraud. Am I deserving of this role when I carry such heavy doubts?

"Thank you," I offer, and they bow, then hurry from my chamber.

Before I can take a peaceful breath on my own, my mother walks in. It's like my chamber is an entertainment hall. Is there a line outside my room of everyone in the palace coming to visit me?

"You look spectacular, just like a king should." She's at my side in moments, her embroidered silk gown as blue as the bright sky. Long-sleeved, her dress carries a high collar and follows her form before falling to her ankles. Small white flowers dot her curled hair, and she wears no crown or tiara, showing she approves of passing the position of Queen to my future bride.

"I'm not ready," I admit out loud.

She steps closer and cups my face. I study the deep lines at the corners of her eyes, the tiredness in her gaze, the grief still clinging to her forced smile. Now that she's lost her husband, it's up to me to care for her. Family is the reason I can't walk away from the throne.

"It's normal to be nervous, Ahren. But you've been preparing for this role your whole life. You just need to be yourself; everything else will fall into place. I'm right here by your side." She beams a glorious smile, and for a few moments, she makes me believe this will be incredible. Then I remember the ache in my chest, the emptiness in my heart, and the unbearable decision I've made.

"Are you ready to become king?" she whispers, the glint of tears collecting in her eyes with pride.

I used to dream about the day someone would ask me that question. Now, I wish more than anything I could turn it down.

Guendolyn

"*P*lease hurry," I gasp.

I lift my head to Michae standing outside my cell, fiddling with a metal key he jabs into the hole. Finally, the door swings open. I run out and throw myself at my guard, wrapping my arms around his neck.

"Thank you, thank you, thank you."

He stumbles and laughs quietly, almost nervously.

"We have no time," he reminds me.

Breaking from him, I nod. "You're right. We have a wedding to stop."

His face blanches. "Umm, that's not what I had in mind. I was thinking of getting away before Jasion can find us, not being incarcerated for challenging royalty."

"You just have to take me to Luther and Deimos, and they will do the rest."

"Yes, miss. Now move quickly and quietly so we can get out of here before the mage returns." He takes the lead, and I stay close behind. Fear bubbles over me with the expectation that any moment now Jasion will curl around the corner of the stairwell. And I worry that Michae alone can't stop him.

Once out of the dungeon, we rush upstairs, my heart banging in my chest. By the time we reach the main door to exit the staircase, I'm breathing heavily.

Michae opens the door, peers out, then waves for me to follow him. I exhale loudly before swinging right to dart down the corridor decorated with animal statues. I've spent so much time in the mansion that I now recognize where we are going… right for the palace.

Abruptly, Michae turns toward me, snatches my arm, and shoves me with him into a room right next to us.

My pulse drums in my veins, and I catch the fear on his face. With the door shut, we both stay silent.

Male voices come from out in the hallway, and when a laugh comes, fire flares over me. It's Jasion.

I inhale softly while I look around the empty room in an attempt to calm myself. I never thought I'd hate someone as much as I do him. Just hearing his voice has my skin crawling. I want to strangle him, except my priority is getting to Ahren. And that means not getting caught by letting anger take me over.

When Michae clicks open the door, I freeze in place as he pops his head out and checks the hallway.

"All clear," he assures me.

I slip out, and we rush forward just as Luther bursts through the door that leads to the bridge between the two buildings.

I don't know who's more shocked—me, who flinches, or Luther, whose eyes practically bulge out of his head.

For a second, we all remain frozen, stunned.

Then I push past Michae and run right at Luther. Throwing my arms around his chest, I press my cheek over his heart and don't let go.

His hands are on my shoulders, and he forces me to look at him. "Little wolf, where the hell have you been? We've been searching everywhere, and I couldn't reach you with my mind."

I meet his gorgeous but worried amber eyes. "Down in the dungeon. Jasion kidnapped me."

His body tenses, his upper lip curling. "I'm going to fucking murder him."

"We don't have time," Guendolyn cuts me off. "I have to stop Ahren's wedding before it's too late."

I stare at her, unsure if this is a result of her not accepting Ahren's decision, or if something else is going on. "You know it's the only way he can claim the throne, little wolf." My heart tightens, as I know this is killing her. "You will always have Deimos and me, baby." I draw her closer by her shoulders, but she brushes me away, anger twisting her lips.

"I know that!" she blurts. "You don't understand. There's so much I have to tell you, and fast. You need to be open-minded, alright?" She looks up and down the hallway as if to ensure we're the only ones around. Michae stands several feet away, but we're otherwise alone.

Leaning in closer, she whispers, "My real father was King Tibout. Eighteen years ago, he had an affair with the queen of Ash Court. I am their child. This is why those in power who know the truth want me dead. Because I'm the rightful heir to both kingdoms."

What the fuck?! My head is spinning. This is nothing like what I expected her to tell me. I was thinking along the lines of her sorrow and deciding she can't live here any longer.

I turn to her. "Where is this coming from?"

She grabs my arm, and I feel her shaking. "When we were at Ash Court to get the cure for Deimos, the king's mother told me about my father, and I should have told you and your brothers right then, but I didn't want to take away from Ahren claiming the throne. He deserves it. That's not what I want..." She pauses, breathing heavily, while my mind reels. "The most important thing here is that if I can show that I am the rightful heir to the throne, Ahren doesn't have to marry someone else."

Except she's wrong. The most important thing here is that she is claiming to be the heir to the throne. But how? "Are you sure?" I ask. "How can you be certain? Did the king say something to you when you spoke to him?" Hundreds of questions barrage my mind.

She blinks at me, confused by my questions, and that's when it occurs to me—if she is the rightful heir to the throne, it won't be Ahren, Deimos, or me in line anymore.

I sit with those thoughts for a while. Since moving to Shadow Court, being a prince has been driven into us and we are reminded of it daily. Told that we would hold great power and positioning one day. And suddenly, we're not.

I'm not sure how to react, but my thoughts are scrambling to make sense of it all. It would explain why she was cursed, why Ash Court wanted her dead, why the rumors and prophecies about her spread so fast in our realm. Were they all intended to make her a target the moment she returned home? All those tales about the curse were used to scare anyone from helping her get back to the Wandering Realm, when in fact the curse on the Shadow Court was because of the king's actions.

Fuck! She might be the heir to both thrones. A spell of dizziness overcomes me.

I swallow hard as I take everything in. "So if

you take the thrones, you are set to inherit the courts from two of the biggest kingdoms in Wandering Realm. You will be the queen of both."

"That's what I just said."

"It only just sank in." I lean against the wall to hold me up. This changes so many things.

"I want you to know I don't want the throne," she admits. "But I can't cope with Ahren being with someone else."

"To be honest," I tell her, "I doubt anyone truly wants that kind of responsibility. Being the king or queen comes with expectations, and it changes you."

She blinks up at me, and I can tell she's trying to understand, but she won't until she takes the position. And as I picture her as queen—my queen—my breath catches in my throat. She will become the most powerful person in this realm when she claims the two thrones.

Fuck!

She doesn't seem to notice my shock and keeps talking. "Also, stupid Jasion sees me as a threat. I heard him conspiring down in the dungeon with an older fae I've never seen before, about how they killed King Tibout and planned to target Ahren to do their bidding."

"Wait! Back up! Jasion killed the king?" I snarl a bit too loud, my heart colliding into my rib cage. A primal growl rips through me—when I see him next, I'm tearing his head from his body with my bare hands. "That sonofabitch. That insignificant rodent has been playing Ahren all along."

"There's more. When I was in the dungeon, I used a portal to escape but ended up in Ash Court. In the Queen's chamber. And that's how I found out she's my mother." She digs her hand down the front of her dress and pulls out a ribbon. She stretches it out, and on it is embroidered her name, Guen. "She gave me this—it's similar to the one that had been on my ankle as a child back on Earth."

I rub my eyes as the truth settles in my mind. I'm still struggling with this news, and the implication is massive. "We need more evidence than just a ribbon." Sure, she's always had a bit of an otherworldly feel about her, and her power with the fairies is very uncommon, but the court will need more to prove she is the rightful heir.

"I know," she whispers, as if it's all too much for her too.

I draw her into my arms, a protective surge

rising through me. I need to keep my little wolf safe from all the monsters who'd harm her.

"Will you help me?" she murmurs, staring up at me. "I need to claim the throne so I don't lose Ahren or any of you. I know how to get evidence to prove who I am… Well, sort of."

"Of course I'll help." There is no other answer.

"Good, then we need to use one of the mages—not Jasion, obviously—to test my blood. My mother said they have a magic test they can perform that can reveal my true heritage."

"I think that's true."

She holds onto my arm. "I have no other choice. We have to do this; it's a risk I have to take."

"I befriended one of the other mages years ago; he can help us. But I need to go stall the wedding or this is all in vain, so Deimos can take you to the mage," I murmur, then turn to Michae. He's my most loyal guard and has done everything in his power to protect my little wolf. "I saw Deimos riding his horse madly near the perimeter of the walls surrounding the castle. Go fetch him urgently."

He taps his chest over his heart twice, bows his head forward, then rushes down the corridor and vanishes around a corner.

"How long before the wedding?" Guendolyn's talking fast, panicking.

"Ahren should be already headed inside, but tradition has it that the new queen must delay her entrance. We don't have much time, but we need Deimos' fast." Even as I'm talking, my mind continues to reel with the news she's dumped on me.

"Will the mages be at the wedding?" she asks, distracting me.

I shake my head. "The old king's mages aren't invited to attend."

"Ouch, that's harsh." She's shaking as she rubs her arms as if cold, and all I want is to wrap her in my arms, for us to talk through what she's just revealed. Her ruling both courts means unity between our kind, the end of war and bloodshed. Mother used to tell me tales about the times when only one kingdom ruled the whole realm, a time when the world lived in the greatest peace in history.

Guendolyn paces in the tight space.

Today's going to go down in history. What my little wolf intends to do will cause an uproar. I can't help but be a little worried, though, because if she's wrong, she will be seen as a traitor, which means a sentence of death I'm not sure even we can stop. But she believes this wholeheartedly, so I have no choice but to believe the same.

I keep glancing at her as she chews on her lower lips. Worry washes over her face, and it hurts to see her so distressed.

"We'll find a way to stop the marriage."

She looks at me like a startled deer, but there's so much more behind those blue eyes. She's gone through such horrific ordeals, and for her to end up in the dungeon must have been terrifying. I tense each time I think about it, and it just drives me harder to destroy everything about Jasion.

"I don't want you to ever think I am doing this to gain power, because I'm not."

"Little wolf." I turn to face her, taking her hand to my lips to place a tender kiss on the back of it, not caring who sees. Nothing will be the same after today. "I don't doubt you for a moment. If that were the case, you would have tried to claim the throne as soon as the king died. Not to mention," I force a cough, "we might not be here right now, as you'd be in there marrying Ahren."

Her expression falls, and she draws her lower lip into her mouth again. "I didn't know the fae rules. I just assumed Ahren would take the throne, not that he had to marry as well. No one told me that part."

I swallow hard, wondering how different things would have turned out if we'd all been open with one another from the start. "You're right. We should have told you right away what was going on. We've all kept things from each other, but that ends here and now. And I also want to know why I can't reach you in your mind anymore?" As I say the words, my energy stretches out to her mind, like I always do when I talk to her, but there's nothing there. It's like I'm lost in a black hole.

"I don't know." She brushes hair out of her eyes and winces.

I catch dried blood on the side of her knuckles. "Show me your hand."

She lowers her hand and looks at her palm. The flesh looks dirty, with dried blood crusted across it.

"What happened?"

"I accidentally smashed the ruby, and shards went into my skin. I think some were still in there when my mother healed the cuts. Ever since the stone broke, I've felt different inside. Could that be why I can't hear your voice anymore in my mind?"

Maybe? I shrug, because I don't have an answer.

This is all so new to all of us. She presses herself against me. She's so small and fragile, and I just want to keep her safe. Except she's a lot stronger than she appears—a lot more than any of us knew, apparently.

"You need to know something. The way I found you on Earth was by using magic… a spell that was initially meant to help me track down my fated mate."

"Fated mate?"

"Yes, we are meant to be together. And I'm convinced it's the same between you and my brothers. Our destinies are intertwined."

She smiles like the admittance is something that brings her joy not surprise. "So, does that mean all three of you, in a perfect world, would be happy to be with me at the same time?" She chews on her lower lip.

"Yes. It's not unheard of in our realm."

Her smile widens and I adore the gleam of excitement in her gaze.

Loud footfalls grab my attention. Deimos marches over to us, arms swinging by his sides, the panic on his face sliding away as he gets closer to us. Michae follows soon after.

"Deimos!" Guendolyn pulls away and runs to

him. They collide, and he embraces her, lifting her off her feet. They kiss, and I smile to see the happiness we inspire in her, and what she's brought out in us.

They fall into a deep conversation, Deimos' face twisting with anger. And by the look of my brother's dropped mouth and the way he freezes on the spot, he's learning about who exactly our little angel is. Must be precisely how I looked when she told me.

"Deimos," I call out, and he twists his head in my direction as I march up to them. "Now that you're caught up, we have to move fast. Take Guendolyn to visit Ramond in the basement and get the blood test done. I have a wedding and coronation to stall for as long as I possibly can without getting tossed into a dungeon myself. Then come to the great hall, fast." My words are rambling, as panic now spins in my chest.

"Why don't you go to your mage friend, and I'll do the distraction," Deimos offers.

"Because the moment Ahren sees you acting up, he'll kick you out. He won't expect it from me. Now go!"

"Thank you," Guendolyn says.

Deimos gives me a begrudging nod, and I see

the questions burning in his gaze. But like me, he knows we don't have the luxury of time if we intend to help Guendolyn.

"Good luck, Luther," he says, and I huff a laugh because if anyone needs luck, it's him and Guendolyn. They're the ones who have to get the evidence to stop the wedding.

I take off and call Michae with me, proclaiming, "Let's go and get into a lot of trouble."

"No matter who you are, you are still my Guendolyn," Deimos states, his fingers squeezing around my hand lightly. That has to be the sweetest thing he's ever said, loving me for who and what I am.

Deimos and I walk hastily through the palace, which is terrifyingly quiet. Only a small handful of guards are here and there.

"You know just the right things to say to make me smile," I answer. "But all this stuff is happening so quickly that I don't have time to really think of the implications. Right now, I'm going on pure instinct, and my priority is to not lose the three fae I want in my life forever."

My thoughts keep swinging back to Luther and

Michae having to stall the wedding. My nerves are tight, worried that they are too late.

Deimos half laughs, drawing me out of my thoughts. He always has that effect on me. I will never get sick of hearing that beautiful sound, either. It always lifts my spirit. "*Stuff* like you being a queen of two kingdoms? Do you know how unheard of that is? Some would say it's impossible."

I shrug as he hurries me down a set of grand marble stairs. Paintings adorn the walls, depicting numerous royal fae in elaborate clothing, in stiff poses that are obviously staged. They are royalty, while I'm… I feel like the lost girl. How can this be my future when I have so much to learn about this realm? Honestly, I didn't even know Ahren had to marry to claim his throne, and that's just one tiny detail of fae culture. So how am I supposed to rule a kingdom?

"There will be portraits of you, too, before long," Deimos tells me, noticing me staring at the past kings and queens of Shadow Court. "You will be stunning."

"Do you think anyone will accept me as their queen? I didn't grow up here." My voice cracks with uncertainty.

Deimos stops in front of me and takes my hands. "They will love you because you will be the Queen of Ash and Shadows."

I eye him. "Is that a real thing?"

He chuckles to himself and drags me back into a fast walk down the rest of the steps. "Just made it up, but I like the sound of it." The smirk he offers is hypnotic. At the bottom of the stairs, he says, "After all of this is done, you and I are spending some serious time together. Just like you and Luther did. Just want to make sure you are aware of that."

He's referring to Luther's proposal to me… I can tell by the way he glances down to the ring on my finger, and despite the mess we're in, he keeps making me smile. "I sure hope so."

"Good." The next thing I know, we're rushing along a darkened corridor that gives me the creeps. Before I can ask any questions, we stop outside an arched doorway, and he bangs his fist on the wood.

The door opens, and we're greeted by a mage I'm not familiar with—then again, I've tried to not pay them too much attention. Like the rest, he's dressed in the usual mage garb, his white hair short and less wild compared to the others. He looks to be in his thirties, his skin tanned like he spends too much time outdoors.

"Your Highness." He bows his head but keeps his eyes on me.

Deimos steps forward. "Ramond, remember that favor you owe me? I'm calling it in."

His face blanches, and he pauses for a few moments before responding. "Shouldn't you be at the wedding?"

"Can you help me or not?" Deimos persists.

The mage stiffens in response. "Of course, Your Highness."

I look past him and into his room, which contains just a simple, small bed, a bedside table, and a wardrobe, with no window. Just candles. This place is depressing, and it almost feels like the mages are put here to be out of sight from others who might fear them.

"Thought so," Deimos answers. "We need to go to your ritual room."

Ramond's brow furrows into dozens of lines in confusion.

"Can you determine someone's heritage through magic?" my prince asks.

The mage stares at me, studying me. Does he recognize me as the princes' healer, like most in the court? I can't help but wonder if he hates me as much as Jasion does.

"I need blood samples, one from the fae being tested and one from the bloodline in question."

His response leaves me frozen on the spot, and Deimos looks at me for a moment, his lips pinched. My mother hadn't said anything about needing a sample from the original bloodline. Then again, she rushed me out of Ash Court fast.

"It's my blood we need to test against King Tibout's," I admit, my insides jittery with worry that they won't have any samples of the king's blood. If he just died, maybe there's a possibility of still getting some from him? The thought turns my stomach, but a wave of desperation constricts around me. "Please, we don't have time."

The mage's eyes narrow. "What's this really about?"

"Listen, Ramond. I heard a rumor that you keep samples of dead royalty blood."

I glance over to Deimos, unsure if he's making this up or it's a fact. And if the latter, why?

"Who have you been speaking to?" His eyes half hood, shadows darkening around him.

"Jasion," Deimos spits.

"Curse him to the Seven Hells," Ramond snarls.

Interesting to see that even the other mages hate Jasion that much.

"Get what you need; we're doing this now," Deimos growls. "I don't care why you have the blood, just fucking take us to it."

Ramond nods. "Your Highness, it's to keep track of bloodlines through history. It helps us trace which lines are the closest aligned to the fairy queen and those of the first fae."

"I don't give a fucking shit!" Deimos snaps, then unleashes a deep exhale. "Get your ass moving!"

Ramond nods, panicked, then hastily emerges from his room and into the hallway.

"This way," he instructs.

Deimos collects my hand, and we're practically running to keep up with the mage, who takes turn after turn down halls where darkness seems to breed. As many questions as I have, I keep quiet, because everything seems to echo here.

The walls are dark stone, and unlike upstairs, there are no paintings. It's depressing here, but the air also feels charged, the hairs on my arms lifting.

At the end of a long corridor, Ramond stops and fiddles with a bunch of metal keys dangling from the chain around his waist, then unlocks a door.

We step into the room, my curiosity piqued by what's inside. Black walls, mostly covered in shelves and shelves of jars filled with powders and liquids in all kinds of colors. Down the middle runs a long table that isn't too different from science labs back home. It smells musty in here, like no one has ever let in any fresh air, ever. The one large window against the back wall is covered by material that has long ago faded to a yellow color, while cobwebs fill the ceiling corners.

Ramond is in the back corner opening a dusty-looking, vintage cabinet. He huffs while jars clang about as he looks for the right blood, I'm guessing.

Deimos' hand squeezes mine lightly, drawing my attention to him. He blows me an air kiss, and I lean against his side. How did I get so lucky to have these princes fall for me? Everything I do now is to hold onto them.

"Found it," Ramond calls out and sets a black vial on the counter, then sweeps back around and heads to the wall covered in floor-to-ceiling shelves. Two seconds later, the whole wall swings open to reveal a hidden compartment.

My mouth drops open, and I peer inside, but only darkness looks back. Ramond vanishes inside.

"Did you know that secret room existed?"

"Of course." Deimos releases his hold of my hand and marches over to investigate. He clearly had no clue.

Just as he pokes his head in, Ramond reappears and Deimos retreats. The mage is carrying a bird-cage large enough to hold a parrot, except he's got a fairy trapped.

My stomach constricts, and I step closer to study the creature fluttering around crazily, trying to escape. It doesn't look well. Its wings are forest green, but the skin on its face and body are sickly pale and streaked with cherry-red veins.

"Why is it imprisoned?" I ask just as the fairy throws itself at the cage, eyes red, mouth gaping open. Razor-sharp teeth bared, it hisses at me. It's nothing like the fairies I've seen before.

"Something's wrong with it!" My insides curdle to see it captured this way.

The mage swings the cage away from me. "It was bitten by a Bloodcursed, but it still holds a lot of power regardless and does the trick, especially since capturing a normal fairy is difficult. By feeding it two drops of different types of blood coupled with the sprinkle of some magic, it will reveal if the blood samples are from the same family or not."

"Bring it all, we need to go. Now," Deimos says as he crosses the room to stand by the door. "I just hope Luther's held off the wedding this whole time."

"We're doing the test at the wedding?" I gasp just as Ramond, carrying everything, rushes past me.

"We need the council and Mother to see the evidence with their own eyes."

I join them quickly as we rush back along the hallway and up the stairs. My breathing speeds up as nerves pinch down my spine. I know Deimos is right, but what if something goes wrong?

Upstairs, we turn onto a wide corridor lit by windows on one side. Farther in the distance are two white doors, like we're about to enter the pearly gates. Is that where the wedding will be held? The thought has goosebumps sprouting along my arms.

I reach over to Deimos just as my sight catches onto a familiar man farther down the hall, talking to several guards. I squint for a better look. White hair, the long coat—I gasp. It's the asshole from the dungeon who conspired with Jasion to kill the king.

My knees buckle as I drown in dread. Deimos

feels me falling behind and turns to face me, his expression swimming in concern.

"What's going on?" he asks.

"It's him." I hate that I try to make myself as small as possible to conceal myself from the man.

Deimos follows my gaze to the older fae, then looks back at me. "Who? My father?"

His words are like a blade slicing at my insides. *Crap!* "That old fae is your real father?" I almost choke on the words. The fucking asshole who ripped Ahren's wings.

When he nods, I suck in a shaky breath. "That's the man who had Jasion kill King Tibout," I whisper. "I heard him praise Jasion for it and say how the bigger they are the quicker they fall, and how they planned to conspire against Ahren to get power in this kingdom. He also intends to relocate to Shadow Court." I try to remember what else I heard while my pulse thumps with adrenaline.

Deimos stiffens, his jawline clenching, twitching. "Are you sure?"

"Yes. The asshole bit my arm." I frantically pull up the sleeve of my dress and show him the ugly mark. "I'll never forget him."

His face burns red like he's about to explode. Fists coiled, he turns from me, but I lunge after him, snatching his coat. "No. Not now. We don't have time right now."

The mage stares at us bewildered, holding onto the fairy that starts screeching in the cage, drawing everyone's attention our way.

Deimos shakes me off and storms over to his father.

My heart beats harder, because this is going to go really bad.

I exchange looks with Ramond, who shrugs like he's used to seeing this kind of drama in the court.

"Fuck, we need to stop him," I say.

I race after Deimos, but before I can get to him, Deimos has lunged himself at his father, throwing him off his feet. Both are on the floor, my prince laying punch after punch into his face.

I should cringe, except I'm cheering on the inside, because his father deserves the worst things in the world. He wanted power, a foothold in this realm, and he got Jasion to take a life. Seething, I tense up, loving every hit Deimos delivers.

Four guards stand around watching for a few moments, probably unsure what to do. After all, Deimos is a prince, *their* prince. Someone who can have them imprisoned for harming him.

Except moments later, two of the guards lunge

forward and heave the prince off his father. "Deimos," I say from behind him. "Please, we need to go."

He faces me, the anger flaring over his expression. I somehow suspect that attack had a lot more to do with how he was treated growing up, more so than just revenge for King Tibout's callous murder or the way I was injured.

He wipes his mouth with the back of his hand. "You're right." His chin lifts to the guards briefly, then he looks down at his father. "Take him to the dungeon and lock him up."

Then he takes me by the elbow and guides me around his father still on the floor, and together with Ramond we close the distance between us and the white doors.

"Halt!" a male's voice calls out from behind us, and we all instinctively glance over our shoulder just as those same guards now march after us with determination.

Deimos' father stands up. He's not being apprehended, he is brushing down his coat and sneering in our direction.

"Take her!" he growls. "She is an assassin! She killed King Tibout!" Seconds later, he darts down a corridor.

What the fuck?

"No!" I recoil. "That's not true."

When Deimos nudges me aside to take a protective step in front of me, I stumble against the mage, both of us teetering while the fairy in the cage goes crazy. Ramond pushes the cage with the fairy into my arms and turns to face the onslaught. Already I can feel the prickle of magic in the air.

The guards slam into Deimos and Ramond, the momentum sending them all crashing against the white doors, creating a tremendous boom. Who the hell are these guards to attack a prince?

A massive man in uniform cracks his neck, straightens his clothes, and saunters toward me with the promise of retribution.

Oh, fuck!

A thunderous boom escapes from behind the doors leading into the main hall, cutting off Luther from his ridiculous singing. A ritual he insists that comes from historic books. I'm not sure if I want to laugh or kick his ass for making a fool of himself in front of everyone.

He sounds like a dying animal. At least the noise has given us a reprieve.

But when the boom doesn't come again, Luther howls another rendition, standing in the middle of the passage that divides the guests into two groups.

Mother glares at me, shaking her head, her perfectly styled white hair bouncing over her shoulders. I hate to see that amount of distress twisting her expression, especially in front of our guests.

"What is he doing?" she hisses.

I know he's stalling, but I can't even begin to understand why. My new bride still hasn't arrived, which I'm guessing is also due to Luther's influence in trying to delay the inevitable.

The great hall is elaborately decorated for the grand wedding of the century. Floral arrangements adorn the white walls, golden vines curl around the marble pillars, while the perfectly white rug that runs down the length of the room is bunched up under Luther where he keeps shuffling about like a madman.

The council members sitting to my right are furious, shifting about, while the guests are more shocked than entertained. The sunlight pouring in from the windows clearly shows every disgruntled face... mostly those from the bride's family.

"This madness is enough," Mother groans in my ear. "End this now before we become the laughing-stock of the realm."

I clear my throat, stand from the throne, and march over to my brother, who's swinging his hands wildly in song about getting drunk before a wedding. He's even coaxed one of his guards to participate with him, who keeps beat by clapping.

We have a great band of talented musicians in the corner who can do nothing but stare on in bewilderment.

Stepping down from the platform where my bride will join me—if she ever arrives—I approach my brother.

He senses me and turns to meet my gaze. The look he gives me is one of pleading for me to back off. In his eyes, I see how hard this must be for him, how he is pushing through this, not for himself… So that means it's for Guendolyn.

Of course that's what this is about. What the hell are they up to? I'm torn, because I want to humor Luther another moment longer to find out where it's going, but the tension in the room is about to explode.

Abruptly, the two doors into the hall burst open, one of them breaking off its hinges, wood splintering everywhere.

Someone screams as two bloodied and bruised guards roll into the room, coming to a stop at the line where the seats begin. They don't move.

The crowd breaks into hysteria, several women yelling with shock.

Deimos strolls into the hall with a bloody lip, his double-breasted doublet ripped at his throat. He's not even dressed in wedding attire. One of the mages he knows, Ramond, joins him, also looking roughed-up with messed up hair, a bruise under his eye, and his necklace sitting over his shoulder.

Behind them enters Guendolyn, carrying a large cage with a fairy fluttering around crazily inside. She looks around sheepish, scanning the enormous room filled with people. When I look outside the room and into the hallway, I find more guards laying on the floor, bloodied and unmoving. Why would the guards fight with Deimos?

I move forward, my heart banging in my ears, waiting for this to somehow make sense. Is this another joke to delay the wedding even further? Fury collects in my chest. This wedding is hard enough as it is; I just need to get it over with. This foolishness ends now.

"What the hell is going on?" I demand.

"Is this no longer a wedding, but a freak carnival?" one of the older council members calls out from behind me.

I stiffen as guards from the room close in on either side of Guendolyn and the mage, then I spot my father slipping into the room, sliding in behind the crowd like he's running late.

"Deimos, what the hell are you doing?" I call out, confused and frustrated. I don't fucking want to marry a stranger, but the throne must be mine to save our family.

My brothers know this.

"Ahren," Deimos begins and Luther steps aside. It seems his part in this ridiculous charade is over. "Before the marriage commences, crucial information has come to light." He wipes the blood from his lip. "King Tibout has a child who is the actual rightful heir to the throne."

The whole room falls silent, and I'm not sure I heard him right. I tense, leaning forward slightly. "What are you saying, brother?" I snarl. What is he doing?

I tense as he takes Guendolyn's hand and brings her forward. Ramond collects the fairy cage from her grasp. She stumbles on her feet and stands before me. The girl I love looks at me with uncertainty, with fear on her face. My insides clench. She's everything I want, my dream, my fantasy, my future… but not in this lifetime, according to fate. Being this close to her does things to me, breaks me over and over to the point I no longer know how to be the fae I once was.

"What in the world is going on here?" my mother says, her footfalls closing in behind me.

"It's true," Guendolyn answers, raising her voice to ensure everyone hears her. "King Tibout is my father. I'm sorry to say this in front of everyone, but the king had an affair with the queen of Ash Court, my mother."

The room breaks out in an explosion of gasps and whispers, and my mother pauses by my side. I'm confused.

"Is this a joke?" I growl.

"Brother." Luther steps forward. "Listen to her."

I turn to my mother, whose face pales as she blinks tears from her eyes. I reach over and wrap an arm around her back. "Come, I'll walk you back to your seat."

She pushes me away and whispers, "I always knew he was seeing that fae, and about the child too, but I accepted it for you three to have a home, a future. I was told she was gone and would never return to the realm."

My throat thickens, and her agony shatters me. Living with such knowledge would have torn her apart, but she did it, nonetheless.

And that means I am not to take the throne today.

"We still loved each other," she admits. "In our own ways. Sometimes you do things in life you don't want for the greater good." She looks at me, clearly referring to me marrying the princess from the east kingdom.

When I stare at Guendolyn and my brothers, a fiery surge of anger rises through me. "You had to wait until now to tell me this? Fucking now?!" Why didn't she tell me earlier? If it's true, I could have married her today and avoided all this.

Betrayal washes over me, because if she cared for me, she would have told me this already. I don't understand… Does she want the throne for herself?

Every eye is on us, every ear taking in the drama that will forever be attached to this kingdom.

"There is evidence for this," the mage who came with them announces. "Well, there will be, once we conduct a test to confirm this girl is indeed, King Tibout's daughter."

The murmurs in the crowd quiet down, and it almost feels like everyone is leaning forward to listen. Mother is right. We will become a joke.

But if Guendolyn is the king's daughter, she has the right to claim the throne before I wed. Though she can't claim it without marrying someone herself.

This is why Luther made a complete fool of himself, isn't it? To help her gain the throne… is he intending to marry her?

Hundreds of questions flood my mind, only adding to my confusion.

Except anger keeps surging within me, growing, while an agonizing heartache spears through my chest. I can't believe Guendolyn and my brothers would keep this from me. I've always been there for them, doing what I think is right. I'm burning up, wanting to demand they tell me the truth.

"This is absurd," Jasion's voice streams across the great hall, tearing me from my thoughts. He's marching toward us from the side of the hall, his jawline clenched tight. Fury flares on his face. What the fuck now?

He reaches my side in moments, his breathing fast. "You cannot allow her to turn this most sacred of ceremonies into a spectacle. If you want to know the truth, it's that she is a spy in our kingdom. I have actual proof that she killed King Tibout."

"That's a lie. Jasion killed the king and conspired with your real father to do it," she shouts.

The shock of her words leaves me speechless. I've started to have doubts about Jasion... but to kill a king?

Deimos flies at Jasion, his punch leading the attack. It clips the mage right in the nose, sending him to the ground in moments.

"What the fuck?!" I grab the back of my brother's doublet and force him away from the mage.

"Has everyone gone mad?" I shout, which does nothing to silence the whispers that spread through the room like wildfire. This is not the venue for secrets to be spilled or accusations to be fired.

Jasion climbs to his feet, blood dripping from his nose. There is no way Guendolyn would kill the king... she was with us when it happened, so that alone confirms Jasion lies. Is he covering up the guilt over the death of the king? I glance over the crowd to where my father sits at the edge, watching with amusement on his face. If there was ever a guilty face, it's that one.

An inferno of anger envelops me at the thought that he had something to do with the king's murder.

Guendolyn steps toward me, but I'm shaking with anger. The repercussions of this will be enormous. Not to mention airing out all of this to all the lords of the kingdom, including my father, who must be beside himself with joy to see us like this from amid the spectators. With the way the bride's advisors glare at me, I doubt this union is happening today. Her and her parents are in a room, waiting to be called for the marriage. And of course, there's the king's sister who sits in the crowd too, waiting like a buzzard to claim the throne. I glance over and find her smirking to herself.

My blood boils, but I can't lose control. That's what everyone expects. What I need is to understand what Guendolyn knows about the murder and how it involves my father and Jasion.

"Can we focus on one thing at a time? If the king has a child, we need proof," one of the council members behind me calls out. "Then we need evidence of who killed the king."

An ache starts at the base of my head and spreads fast, the stress mounting by the second.

I turn to the mage grasping the cage with the fairy. "Show us the evidence. And be fast about it. My patience is running out."

"Your Highness," Jasion insists, his voice loud and clipped. "You can't seriously be entertaining this. She murdered King Tibout."

I swing around and grab him by the throat, drawing him to me. I'm barely holding onto any semblance of sanity, and this asshole pushes me by counting on me not knowing he lies.

"Be very careful what you say when I know you're lying," I growl.

His face goes as white as snow, but then I witness his expression morph into confidence within moments, like that's all it takes for him to reconstruct his story. I've always thought he was a friend, but that was a huge mistake on my part. I see that now. I release him, and he stumbles on his feet. Once this is over, I will personally interrogate him. I look over to my guards to call them over when Jasion's voice sears across the room to ensure everyone hears.

"Your Highness," he continues, and my fingers twitch into fists. "Surely you are aware that permitting someone to challenge the claim to the throne comes with repercussions. If this girl, *this assassin*, cannot prove she is the rightful heir, then she will face death in her attempt to usurp the throne."

I swing toward him, my fists tight. His words sucker-punch me right in the gut. I glare at him, picturing how I will destroy him. "You are not—"

"Agreed," my mother calls out from behind me. "Get this absurdity done, then everyone who disrupted this ceremony will be interrogated and face the harshest of punishments. This is enough!"

The crowd cheers in a kind of maddening approval. I look at my mother, infuriated that she's siding with Jasion. But at the same time, I can't begin to imagine how hard this must be for her. To lose a husband she knew cheated on her, then to have his child come to claim the throne from me. To be reminded of his infidelity.

"Guards," I bellow. "Apprehend Jasion and lock him up in the dungeons."

The mage's face falls as two guards from the side of the room carry out my order. Fury twists Jasion's face, hatred pouring from him, but I can't stand to look at him another moment. I curse him under my breath and vow that once this is over, he will be tossed to the Bloodcursed for all I care. No interrogation needed—his fate is sealed in Shadow Court.

I glance over to Guendolyn, who's chewing on her lower lip, fear building behind her eyes. She meets my gaze, and my first instinct is to pull her into my arms, to take her out of here and get her to tell me everything. But I don't move, because that's not going to work. Not when hundreds of fae are invested in this scandal. The only way to douse the flames is with a public display of the truth.

My mind is foggy as I contemplate Guendolyn's intention to take the throne as queen. I won't deny, at the back of my mind, I ask myself if part of her motive is to make me suffer after I pushed her away. To take away the one thing I picked over her…

I shake my head. She wouldn't do that.

My thoughts linger to when we were last together on the balcony and she healed my wings. To her torn expression when I turned her down.

Why didn't she tell me about her ancestry before?

A loud clap draws my attention to my mother. "Perform your test up here for all to see." She's furious and won't even look at me. She fears losing our home if the test proves truthful, not to mention the wolves within the crowd ready to pounce.

The mage carries the cage up the steps and stands in the middle of the stage, looking toward Mother and the council. I move to take a seat alongside her, while my brothers come to stand on either side of us.

Guendolyn climbs the stairs, holding her head high. For her sake, I pray the test proves she is who she claims to be. Not being with her is one thing, but to have her executed will end me. The ache in my gut returns, the muscles in my shoulder blades pinching with stress. It's snowballing, and each breath comes out ragged.

I sit next to Mother, my whole body tense as shit, and I wait. Guendolyn looks so nervous. It's difficult to watch her this way when I want to protect her from everyone—except she's asking to be at the forefront of everything.

She hid this secret from me. It didn't have to end up this way.

"Ramond, you may commence," Deimos instructs.

The mage nods once and sets the cage on the

floor near his feet. "I don't carry a blade on me," he says. "I need a few droplets of blood from..." He glances over to Guendolyn, clearly not knowing her name.

"G-Guendolyn," she says softly, her gaze traveling to us before returning to the mage. There are gasps through the room, even my mother's breath catches at learning who stands before her. The cursed girl from our realm.

The mage doesn't seem to bat an eye and pulls out a small wooden bowl the size of my palm from the pocket of his robe-skirt.

I stand and draw a blade from my waist, then approach her. She gingerly offers me her hand palm side up, the mage gripping the bowl close to catch the blood.

She's soft to the touch, and I feel her trembling. "It's going to hurt just for a bit," I whisper.

"It's alright," she reassures me. Like it's me who needs comfort when her life is at risk. I don't even know if I'll be able to help her if she's accused of treason and sentenced to death. And I struggle to breathe at the thought.

"Are you sure this is what you want to do?" I hesitate a bit, speaking softly so the others don't hear.

She blinks up at me with the same heartache in her eyes she carried on the balcony. "There's nothing else I want more than to be with you."

The mage next to us clears his throat, but he remains in place with his bowl. My breath catches, and all the emotions I've shoved deep inside me burst to the surface. The ones that insist I walk away and just follow my heart. To claim the girl in front of me, to be happy for once in my fucking miserable life.

That's when I realize she doesn't want the throne for herself, but to ensure I take it with her.

My throat thickens, and I don't move. Not when I see everything she's going through for me.

"Do it," she whispers. "Please. Just cut me."

Silence permeates the room, everyone seeming to wait with bated breath.

So much rides on this, so many people's lives and futures.

"I hope you're right." I make a quick swipe over the meaty part of her palm, the blade biting into her flesh. Blood bubbles quickly along the cut. She tilts her hand to the side as red droplets roll down her palm and trickle into the bowl.

When a small puddle is collected, the mage says, "That's enough."

Guendolyn pulls back, and I hand her the handkerchief from my pocket. I tuck my blade away and return to my seat. My gut tightens, and with each passing moment, unease curls inside me. I feel like I'm about to watch the world's biggest disaster, and I'm doing nothing to prevent it.

I glance over to Luther, who gives me a reassuring look like we are doing the right thing. How can he be so sure?

The mage retrieves a small black vial from his pocket, uncorks it, and starts pouring what looks like someone else's blood in with Guendolyn's. "This is King Tibout's blood," he announces.

Not a single word can be heard from the packed room. The silence is strangling me.

Once he has the vial closed and back in his pocket, he crouches by the cage.

The fairy inside sits against the back wall, silent, watching him with huge eyes. Opening the small latch at the side, he quickly slides the bowl into the cage before retracting his hand. A light blue energy stretches from his fingers to the bowl, vanishing as quickly as it came.

He lifts the cage and turns toward us. "This fairy has been bitten by a Bloodcursed, and with my magic, when it drinks the blood, it will react in one of two ways. It will either sit calmly, which will tell us the bloods are from the same bloodline. Or it will go ballistic, crashing into the walls to escape, as it'll be momentarily poisoned by the mixed blood."

Guendolyn stands nearby, pressing the hand-kerchief to her cut, and like the rest, her eyes are glued to the cage.

The fairy wanders over to the bowl, where it drops to its knees. In the silence of the room, the fairy lapping the blood is all that's heard.

Moments later, it jerks its head up.

Guendolyn hugs herself, and I can't move. I'm frozen in my seat, waiting, desperate to see this succeed. *Please, let this work.*

The sudden explosion of the fairy's wings shooting outward on either side of her, green as moss and beating frantically, causes my heart to race and a terrible ache to sweep through my gut.

The fairy starts spinning mid-air inside the cage, faster and faster. She isn't bouncing about crazily though, but remains in one spot, whirling around.

"What does that mean?" I demand.

The mage licks his dry lips and glances over to me. "I've never seen this before."

A gasp falls from Guendolyn's lips, and the whole room bursts into sound. It isn't long before a few start demanding her death.

My heart beats frantically, and I try to curl in on myself, wanting to vanish right here and now. My gaze darts between the spinning fairy in the cage and the perplexed mage as the chants for my death escalate.

These fae don't even know me, yet they want me dead? How in the world are they meant to embrace me as their queen when they're tossing me aside so hastily?

Power flares down my arms. It's getting to the point where I don't care about the throne; I don't care about anything but trying to be with my princes. Maybe the answer lies in me taking all three with me to Earth and make a go of things there. But that'd be running away from my problems, wouldn't it?

I approach Ramond and whisper, "Can we try again, please?"

He looks at me with sympathy and nods. Ramond, thankfully, is nothing like Jasion.

Luther and Deimos step forward, while I hold Ahren's gaze. They support me, but he must have doubts that I'm not telling the truth—otherwise, why does he hesitate?

I try to think if my mother said anything else about how to do this, anything we may have missed the first time around. I can't stop trembling, fearful of what will come next.

Luther comes up to me and leans down to whisper in my ear. "Let Deimos and I take you from here safely."

I lift my head and look into his eyes. "You believe me, don't you?"

"Yes, but it's not about us, little wolf. Right now you're in danger. Please," he whispers, his tone shaken.

The sound of something clanging draws my attention to Ramond, who's taking the small bowl out of the fairy's cage. The moment he does, the poor fairy collapses to the ground. It crawls over the side of the cage toward me and grabs the metal bars, staring at me with the most heartfelt eyes. No longer does it look wild and ready to tear into anyone who gets too close. It's calmer, and all I feel is pity for the little thing.

"Guendolyn," Luther persists in my ear.

I face him. "Please, let me try one more time. Give me that."

There's no hesitation. He nods, and I have to resist the urge to hug him. I need to be strong and appear in control, even though inside I'm filled with turmoil.

Luther addresses the royals and council. "Now that our initial trial is complete, we will proceed with the actual test."

Jasion groans loudly. "She is a traitor, and you are openly allowing her to betray you." Why the hell isn't he in the dungeon like Ahren ordered? Several others in the crowd start echoing his words, which was exactly his intention.

"Luther," the queen warns.

The prince addresses everyone in the room. "I don't know about the rest of you, but when someone claims to be a lost heir, it is our duty to give them every chance to prove their stake. If

King Tibout were alive, he'd agree, and everyone here knows it." He turns to a guard.

"She's bewitched the prince. You all can see she failed the test. We don't need more proof. She killed the king and now she's trying to take the throne."

"Gag and tie up Jasion now!" he roars.

A guard snatches Jasion and forces him to a seat, tying him up and gagging him.

"My Queen, this has gone on long enough. Please, I implore we push ahead with the ceremonies," a male intones from behind me. It's one of the councilmen, an old, stuffy fae. The others around him nod their heads.

Voices from all around start to rise as everyone chats amongst themselves. Sweat drips down my back, and I swallow hard. The councilmen break into an argument, and the realization of how horrible this is going sinks through me.

I look back to the fairy and reach over to stroke its wing inside the cage. It doesn't look crazed any longer but more like a fairy who's lost, and I'm left wondering if feeding it my blood has had this effect.

"Let it out," I say to Ramond, but he doesn't

hear me and is staring wide eyed at something at the entrance to the hall.

An explosion of panicked voices booms from the crowd as attendees scramble away from their seats and spread outward in the room.

Emerging through the doorway is my mother. My mouth drops open. She's wearing a pale blue gown glinting with diamonds, her hair pinned off her face with a glittery crown, lips rosy and bright. She's beautiful. Stunned is an understatement on how I feel. What is she doing here?

Behind her, half a dozen guards in the dark uniform of the Ash Court march in tight formation.

"Mother!" I call out, gaining everyone's stare. The way Ahren looks at me in shock resembles his brothers' expressions as they tried to comprehend who exactly I am, reminding me that Ahren hasn't heard this part of my story yet.

In fact, everyone glares at me that way, disbelief and confusion about how I could be both the daughter of a Seelie and an Unseelie running rampant.

She smiles at me, but before she can speak, someone else steps forward.

"Son," Ahren's father emerges from the

cowering masses. "I can't sit back any longer and watch this embarrassment. You are in over your head. It's clear that witch has invited the enemy into our court, and yet you still haven't summoned her arrest?! Has she bespelled you, or is her cunt truly made of gold!"

Deimos throws himself off the stage to lunge at his father, roaring like a beast, face contorted with fury. Luther and Ahren on his heels, seizing him by the arms to hold him back. But by the raging anger twisting their expressions, at first I can't tell if they are stopping Deimos so they can get to their father first and beat the hell out of him.

"Fuck you!" Luther spits, gaining gasping shock from the guests.

This is turning into a spectacle, and their fucking asshole father has to make a show, doesn't he? I steel myself and glare at him, my hands curling into fists. I'm furious at his words, but at the same time panicked at the mounting tension in the room.

"Apprehend the queen!" Ahren's mom bellows, rising from her throne, drawing away from the explosive thickness in the air.

"No!" I cry out, lunging for the steps to reach my mother's side.

"Is that the welcome I get after I had my mage end the curse on your kingdom, under duress mind you? The creatures are no longer lured to your kingdom. They're still around eradicating them completely is a lot more complicated, but the mage with his dying breath was able to stop their bites from transforming anyone into a Blood-cursed." My mother's eyebrow arches, and the whole room gasps. These creatures have plagued these lands for a long time from what the princes had told me, so this is amazing news. "I did it for my daughter, for your kingdom to embrace her, and I risked everything for this to work."

Someone claps in the crowd, then more follow, standing up because she has eradicated a huge problem.

But when a sudden spark booms in the room from our right, everyone flinches with fright. I smell electricity in the air. Magic, to be more precise.

The Shadow Court guards draw their swords in unison and I flinch from the abrupt, ringing sound. They appear stiff, their eyes pale, glazed over like zombies… like they are being controlled.

"Ahren, son, you must be able to see through their ploy to take your throne from you. King

Tibout is dead so he can't dispute this. But even I can see it clearly what is happening here."

"This has nothing to do with you, Father," Ahren growls.

One of the guards slashes the cords binding Jasion's wrists and gag, and he's up on his feet, joining the princes' father. They sneer, looking at me. "Change of plans," Jasion declares as more guards dart into the ballroom from the hallway, blocking off everyone's exit. And that's when it hits me that this is all Jasion's doing and why the guards don't apprehend him. He had this orchestrated from the beginning.

"Guards, stand down," Ahren commands, Deimos and Luther moving to his side and drawing their blades. Their mother, along with the councilmen, recoil to the rear of the stage. But no one listens… They are under Jasion's control now.

Fear lifts the hairs on my arms. This is going to turn into a bloodbath.

"It didn't have to be this way," his father says. "But maybe this is what this kingdom needs. A clean slate and a new beginning. A new king in charge."

"Father! This has nothing to do with you," Ahren snarls.

But with a single whistle from Jasion, the guards charge, attacking anyone in their way—Shadow and Ash Court alike—as they carve their way toward us.

The screams are ear-shattering, and dread shakes me at the core. Instinct and panic take over, and I race down the aisle to my mother as she runs to me. Fear tightens her face even as she hurls her arm outward, a blast of power colliding into a guard coming for her, tossing him into the hoard of soldiers. She gasps and slows down suddenly. I take her arm.

"I'm not as strong as I once was," she says amid the chaos.

"We need to get you out of here," I shout, grasping my mother's hand, drawing her toward the stage while my three princes and Michae leap into battle alongside the Ash Court guards.

Screams and chaos spread like wildfire. The clang of metal resonates, while fear strangles my heart.

And there it is. As soon as something good is about to happen, the universe says, *Fuck you!*

The air thickens with hatred and death so fast it leaves my head spinning.

"Your Majesty," I address the princes' mother. "Stay close. I'm going to get you both out of here."

I'm shaking furiously as I call to the power inside me. I stare at the palm with shards of ruby inside. *Please work.*

"I'm Queen Sarey," my mother says to the queen, who looks torn, her eyes glinting with tears. "This isn't the best circumstance for us to meet, but please know I have always held the highest respect for you."

"Oh? Did you respect me when you were sleeping with my husband?" she spits while more people run onto the stage, crying.

Shit, this isn't the time for this.

"After Guendolyn, we stopped seeing each other. He truly loved you," my mother explains, stretching her hands out to the queen. "I wish I would have come to you earlier and explained it all."

But I don't have time for this.

Just as I realize I've lost track of where my princes are in the fight, Luther is tossed across the floor, blood streaking his cheek. Jasion throws a ball of energy at the guards standing in his way, while the princes' father pushes a woman out of his path so can he reach the stage faster.

My pulse is a raging storm. Ramond is at the edge of the stage, looking like he's attempting a spell on the battle, except mages need the proper ingredients to empower their magic. Whatever he does will be weak, but at least he's trying. Near him sits the fairy in the cage. And a better idea comes to me.

I lunge for the cage and fumble with the door, opening it. The fairy flutters out instantly, its wings wide and beautiful.

"Please will you help me?" I cry out, outstretching my hand that has the ruby embedded.

As if understanding, it flutters and lands on my wrist.

The princes' mother gasps from behind me. "You have the power of the fairies?"

"Yes," my mother explains. "Just like my ancestors. This is why she is the rightful heir to not only the Shadow Court throne, but the Ash Court throne as well. You don't have to like it, but deep down inside, you know it's right."

The princes' father charges onto the stage, pushing others aside and coming at me so fast I don't react quickly enough. His fist finds the side of my face, and I see stars as I fall backward with a thump.

Wings flutter in my face, and a hissing fills my ears.

"You will ruin everything," he snarls. His shadow towers over me, and I open my eyes as the fairy flings itself to his face, scratching and biting him. He bats at the fairy like a lunatic.

My mother throws her arms toward him, and the fairy flings away from him in that same moment.

An explosion of air punches the old fae in the chest, and he's hurled across the room where he slams into a pillar. He groans and slumps to the ground, and I do a small cheer on the inside.

My mother stumbles on her feet as if suddenly exhausted, barely catching her breath. The queen of Shadow Court catches her around the waist. "I have you."

I get to my feet, trying my best to ignore the pain flaring down my face like it's on fire and concentrate instead.

"Take everyone as far back in the corner as you can." I gesture the queens toward the part of the stage where the gutless councilmen hide like rats.

My mother helps keep everyone together behind me, as far from the danger as possible.

The fairy returns to my outstretched wrist once more. The battle spreads to my left, guards against guards, princes, and some of the guests who've harnessed knives to fight against the possessed soldiers.

I can't see Jasion anywhere, but I don't have time for that right now.

Energy flares down my arms and I lift the fairy closer to my face. It mimics me, and we both blow a breath onto our palms. Blue haze spills past my lips.

"Fairies," I whisper, and my little friend makes a sound that sounds very close to *Eirian*.

In seconds, a black portal spreads out before me, growing in size. My skin ripples with goosebumps from the power. The sounds of battle and screams surround me, but I try to focus on what I've opened, praying this works. My fairy takes off and vanishes right into the portal. Oh, crap. That wasn't the plan. Maybe I'll get all the guests to do the same.

A sudden punch drives into my lower back with such force, all the air is knocked out of my lungs and my legs buckle. I drop to my knees, gasping, arching my back from the ache zigzagging up my spine.

An arm locks around my throat and wrenches me to my feet and up against a hard chest. "Got you, bitch!" Jasion snarls in my ear, strangling me.

I struggle against him, shoving my elbow into his gut and kicking my heel into his shin. "Let me go!"

His grip tightens. "You will die today!"

Dread shudders through me.

"This is something I should have done long ago." He raises a blade over my chest.

My life flashes before my eyes, and with it comes visions of everything that will be ripped from me. This piece of scum will kill those who mean everything to me and take away what I've fought to find my whole life—my family and happiness.

When I catch sight of Ahren pinned to the ground by two guards, Deimos is surrounded by three others, and Luther is thrown into a wall, my heart bleeds.

I draw on everything inside me, every thread of power, and call it to the surface just as I had back in Ash Court.

A blast of energy launches from my hands so

feprociously that I'm suddenly shoved back into Jasion, both of us stumbling. His grip loosens, and I pivot on my feet, driving my palms against his chest. All the power inside me pummels into him.

He's thrown backward and onto his back in an instant.

His eyes widen into orbs, the blade drops from his grip, and he glances down to his chest. Blood seeps from where my energy hit him. A terrifying cry spills from his mouth as he frantically wipes as more and more blood emerges from his pores.

An explosive flutter of air zooms right past me on both sides.

Wings are all I see at first, violets and greens and magenta, then I make out the dozens of fairies —no, hundreds of fairies—swarming through the great hall.

I yelp with joy at seeing them—they are the most incredible sight.

A group rushes over and attacks Jasion, surrounding him until they coat his entire body. His screams are all I hear, while wings beat around him.

Maybe I should feel pity, but the vindication of giving him exactly what he deserves is the sweetest satisfaction ever. After just a few moments they pull back from their assault, leaving behind the clattering of bones falling to the floor. Clothes. Hair. And a few flecks of blood.

That is all that remains of the fucking asshole mage, and even that is too much. I'm going to make sure every bit of him is burned to ashes.

The guests at the far end of the stage are crying out, ducking from fairies who aren't even touching them. My mother stands before them, looking at me with a wide, approving grin. "Finish this," she says.

A fairy with glinting blue wings flutters in front of me and waves.

I blink to clearly see, and my heart beams. "Hiss!" I can't stop smiling because this little critter is exactly who I'd hoped to call. "You came!"

Eirian. The word streams over my mind, and she swings around and hisses, pointing to the chaos.

I turn to the hall where the Shadow Court guards are no longer fighting but cowering away, falling to their knees before the princes with remorse, with confusion. Which confirms that Jasion did indeed spell them.

Dead bodies litter the floor, fae who lost their

lives because of two greedy bastards. And my sights set on the princes' father, slithering like the snake he is to dart out of the room. "Hiss, bring him to me."

She catapults across the room like a torpedo, an arrow of fairies right behind her.

They collide into him, taking him off guard.

He spins around, his face contorted in panic as he sees what's coming for him. His screams are music to my ears.

The gorgeous little creatures swarm him as he fights against them, flinging his arms out, but he's off his feet in seconds. They carry him over to me, then drop him down where he collapses onto his knees in front of the steps before me.

My three princes approach their father, as does his ex-wife. My mother is by my side.

"Ahren," he grovels. "Will you let her hurt me? I'm your father, your flesh and blood."

My prince steps up to his father, his expression one of pure hatred and fury. He lifts his fist and drives it into his father's face, sending him to the floor on his back. "I no longer have a father."

Ahren then unbuttons his jacket and lets it drop to the floor behind him, followed by pulling his top up and over his head.

The Queen on the stage gasps, but I know exactly what he's doing, and I love him for this.

His shoulders curve forward as the back of his shoulder blades split downward. Wings push out of his back, the sound like leather rubbing together. They spread out on either side of him in glorious blues and violets and white. Spanned outward, they a large portion of the room's width. My prince lifts his chin, not ashamed of what his father told him was wrong, and I'm so fucking proud of Ahren.

The whole room is oohing because their prince has the most spectacular wings, which I believe is rare.

He glares down at his father and says, "You tried to break me, but it didn't work. Fuck you!"

He glances at me and gives me a nod of approval, as do Deimos and Luther. I glance over to their mother, who is red in the face with fury. "Kill him!" she demands.

I smile while the worm writhes, crying for escape.

"He's yours, Hiss." I point to him, and the fairies descend on the old fae in seconds.

They are ruthless, biting, tearing skin, gouging holes in his face and body. I refuse to look away, because if I intend to take my role in this realm, I must show strength.

My princes stand by, watching the man who brought so much grief to their lives finally get what he deserves. Though in truth, I do feel like they are killing him a bit too fast. This should be elongated, drawn out a bit more.

The slurping and chewing sounds are muffled by the terrified sounds of the guests. Yep, this is definitely not the wedding that was planned. I somehow doubt anyone will ever forget today. Ahren draws back his wings, and gets dressed, and I catch the smirk on his face. This is something so long overdue for him.

Most in the audience don't know where to look... him or the ruthless end to a horrible fae.

My mother comes to my side along with Ramond, carrying his bowl of blood.

"It's time they saw the truth so you can take your rightful place," my mother reminds me. She grasps a blade and runs the sharp end down her palm in a quick swipe. She turns her hand sideways and lets her blood drip into the bowl that still holds blood from King Tibout and me.

Ramond runs his hand over the liquid, blue energy covering the surface. Then he offers the bowl to Hiss. "This will work on any fairy," he reassures us.

Hiss looks at me, and I nod, praying this time goes better than the last.

My heart beats frantically. Nerves zip up my spine with worry that this will fail.

I remember when I was small, and I once had to wait for blood test results because they feared I might be epileptic. The wait was excruciating. But that doesn't come close in comparison to this. This is a hundred times worse.

Ahren's face is stoic, eyes glued to Hiss, who lands on the mage's arm and leans in, tasting the blood. Seconds later, she is feverishly lapping at the offering.

Her head suddenly jerks up, mouth covered in blood, more dripping from her chin. Her eyes are wide like she's tripping on something really good.

I want to shut my eyes and turn away so I don't have to watch this. All I can picture in my mind is her bursting about wildly. Coldness floods me, and it chills me at the core. My knees tremble.

The fairy dunks her face back into the dish, loving every drop.

My mother takes my hand in hers and leans

over. "There is nothing you need to fear. Ever again."

Suddenly, the little critter pulls her head up, and several people in the room gasp in anticipation.

I hold my breath, watching her surge into clumsy flight toward me, her wings stretching out, twitching. The more I look at her, the more I expect her any second now to burst into a frenzy.

My mother grasps my arm.

And I hold my breath while we wait.

CHAPTER 20

AHREN

Every inch of me aches, including where I'd been kicked in the balls by a fucking guard. But now I can't move as I follow every stiff, jutting movement the fairy makes.

This day will go down in history—the entire realm will talk about this—but all I care about is keeping Guendolyn safe. If she'll have me, I'll take my place by her side.

The fairy suddenly drops out of the air and lands clumsily on Guendolyn's shoulder. Finding her balance, the fairy settles down on her knees. Her head tilts downward, and she begins to snore softly. Guendolyn collects her into her arms, while the rest of the fairies surround us and watch.

"It's a match," Ramond announces loudly,

making everyone flinch. "Guendolyn is the daughter of King Tibout of Shadow Court and Queen Sarey of Ash Court. She is the rightful heir to both kingdoms."

No one dares speak or even move with that announcement, and I'm bursting with joy on the inside. I want this for her more than I could have ever thought. "Oh Guendolyn," I say and move to her with haste. "This is everything you deserve."

Guendolyn gasps, her expression one of shock, as if she can't believe her ears. With glistening eyes, she wraps her arms around my middle, and I embrace her, kissing the top of her head.

My mother looks at me strangely.

"This is who I want to marry," I declare loud enough for all to hear. "If her and the Queen of Ash Court will have me."

"Yes," she answers. "I want to marry all three of you."

There are gasps from the crowd, but it isn't an uncommon event for a queen or king to take more than one partner to rule alongside them. My brothers join us, and I've never been so happy. I never expected to find this kind of joy amid death, never expected that somehow I'd find a way out of the corner I'd been wedged into.

I glance over to where the guests are dispersing around the room and catch the eye of the advisors from the kingdom to our east. I was meant to marry their princess, yet they stare at me with anger burning in her eyes. My first point of call is to address this with them and apologize for how today has turned out. I wave over to my advisor, Mael and instruct him to take our guests from the east to where Queen Titania, her husband and daughter wait in the castle. "I won't be long and don't let them leave." It's a hard conversation I am hoping I can smooth over for the sake of our relations.

"Of course." He bows his head and rushes away. I hate that they've been put in this situation, but I won't change that I finally got what I wanted.

The queen of Ash Court says, "This test confirms Guendolyn's true legacy as a descendant of two royal lines. And by the looks of our winged friends, my little girl also has the fairy queen's power." She clears her throat and looks over to my mother and then the council, who stand amid the crowd of guests, huddled and utterly shocked.

I'm still dealing with learning that Guendolyn is the princess of both Shadow and Ash Courts... and now, added to that, she is now also the queen of the fairies. My mind can barely comprehend this turn of events. If anyone deserves this, it's my Guendolyn.

"There is more," the queen says. "Many know my daughter as the cursed girl in our realm, but not many understand she was cursed as an infant by my mother-in-law and husband so that she would never return to our realm to claim the thrones and to unite our kingdoms. I was never given a choice and did what I could to protect my girl, which is why I hid her amid humans in the Earth realm. But now that she is back, I want to bestow a gift upon her for all the wrongs done against her. To make things right."

She moves to take her daughter's hand. "My bloodline is of the original family that came from the fairy queen herself. I was forced into a loveless marriage. Now I am taking a stand. I am officially abdicating my position as Queen of Ash Court. The throne is open to be claimed by a family member as I have stepped away. And my husband can't do anything about it as you are the heir by blood." She glances over to Guendolyn, who is crying happy tears.

My stomach knots up, because this is unprecedented. No royalty has ever renounced their throne. Deimos' mouth drops open, while Luther blinks in disbelief.

"Mother," Guendolyn whispers, her voice shaken. She draws away from me and rushes into her arms.

My heart warms to finally see Guendolyn find her family, to know where she belongs. I grew up loathing what my father did to me, so focused on becoming a better king, on what changes I'd need to make in order to achieve some semblance of happiness in the future, that I didn't see that I already had everything I needed. It took a while, but with Guendolyn, we got there. And there's nothing I would ever change… though I do wish the path here wasn't so treacherous or heart-breaking.

I turn to my mother and collect her in my arms, as do my brothers.

"Looks like we have another wedding to plan?" she says, tears pooling in her eyes, glancing up at me, smiling like she used to when life was easier.

"And you're fine with the union between the kingdoms, with us three marrying her?" I ask.

"Of course. I lived too long with hatred; now I just want peace, and grandchildren. And if this brings my three boys what I couldn't have, then I give my blessing."

"About time!" Deimos calls out, drawing everyone's attention.

Guendolyn glances over and laughs like she can't believe this is happening. The rest of the guests and councilmen are silent, clearly lost for words.

I step aside from my family and kneel in front of my queen, my brothers following suit.

"Guendolyn, to make it official, will you have us three as your husbands as you claim the thrones?" I ask, wishing I had a ring to offer her.

The way she looks at us is heart-warming, and a tear slips down her cheek. "Absolutely. It's why we did all this. So we can all finally be together."

In that same moment, the fairies break out into a beautiful song and begin fluttering around the room in a splendid aerial dance.

My heart thumps, and adrenaline races through my veins. We have found our queen. This is the day I've dreamed of... to get what I want in the end. Never believed it could happen, but now that it's here, I will fight to the end to ensure it remains. We will prove ourselves to her.

I tilt my head as she kneels in front of us and

she embraces us all saying, "Please tell me this isn't a dream?"

We all burst out laughing, and I lean in to brush my lips over hers. I try to act casual, to pretend my heart isn't pounding in my chest and that I want to scream at the top of my voice that she's mine. Instead, I just whisper, "This is only the beginning of your new life."

CHAPTER 21

GUENDOLYN

One Day Later

I'm in my room in the mansion, staring out the window at the landscape. The rolling hills and woodlands coated in snow, the superb sunlight brightening the blue sky, the land-scape that I reign over. Me, the lost girl who only wanted to find her family, but instead, I found something more incredible than I ever thought possible.

The notion of who I really am and what this means still doesn't feel real, but I haven't been able to stop smiling or spinning around on the spot each time I think about how things ended up.

I recall a corny saying about how when life gives you lemons, you give it lemonade back. Well, I've just created the fucking golden ambrosia of the gods' kind of drink with my lemons.

Don't get me wrong... I'm nervous as hell to become a Queen. But I get to be with my three princes unquestionably now, and that is what I really care about.

Yesterday's events at Ahren's wedding to a princess turned into a whirlwind. Everyone keeps telling me, the day will go down in history, talked about across the realm, and my name will be on their lips. The cursed girl who will become Queen. Songs will be written about me, and in truth, that just makes me laugh because it can't be me they are talking about.

The princes had assured me, they are by my side and I will make a strong leader, and while I believe them, the trepidation that I will fail everyone drags heavily through me.

So, I escaped to my room where it's quiet. After all, the princes have been dealing with the guests who came to our court from far away kingdoms for a wedding that never happened, not to mention the princess and her family. Everyone has been welcomed to remain a few extra days so they may attend the real wedding.

A buzz runs down my spine at the thought of my marriage, and those butterflies spring up in my stomach. This is happening.

This is actually happening.

Goosebumps cover me with elation.

A knock at the door has me spinning around to find Michae in the doorway, hands stiff by his side, a relaxed expression on his face. "Prince Ahren has requested your presence." He bows his head forward. "He has something to show you."

"For me?" My nerves start dancing beneath my skin.

Michae smiles calmly, reassuring me. Then he gives me a cheeky grin. "Shall we go, my lady?"

I follow him out into the hallway where it's quiet. Majority of the staff are in the palace to clean up after yesterday. Others are helping with my wedding. Apparently, I don't get a say in how it runs. Under Fae customs, it's up to the mothers of the bride and groom to arrange all the whole event. I am hoping this means my mother and the princes will start to get along.

Michae walks me through the mansion, over

the bridge and soon brings me to a small enclosed courtyard with a clear ceiling to view the sky. The castle walls surround the gardens on four sides. Flowering trees of pinks and whites dot the land. Roses and flowers scatter in between, along with shrubs. There's a small vegetable garden to my right, and even a round marble fountain, spouting water. This is a greenhouse, and it's spectacular.

Half a dozen butterflies flutter through the air, and I already want to move my bed here.

"Follow the path," Michae tells me, and when I turn toward him, he's retreating inside and shuts the door.

There's only exhilaration in my veins. The two fae from the court who wanted me dead are gone, and I doubt Michae would put me in danger after everything we'd all experienced recently.

I take a step forward, then another over the cobblestones dotting the ground, while flowers of every color surround me while the butterflies sweep around. I pass trees with gold and red globes like apples, the air heavily perfumed with lilac and vanilla scents. I feel like Alice in Wonderland, my stomach a buzz with adrenaline of what I'll find. And why haven't I been taken to this garden before? Only once I curve around a large weeping tree, does a wooden hut with a pointy roof come into view. No windows, but there's an open doorway.

Curiosity has me lifting my deep red dress that dances around my ankles and hurry forward.

Stepping up to the doorway, I meet Ahren inside, sitting on a black leather chaise lounge that looks more like it belongs in the throne room, rather than as garden furniture. My prince stands at my presence, his smirk captivating. White long hair is combed and parts just over his temple. Full lips pull into a devious grin, while those jeweled green eyes draw me closer. There is a different air about him today. Gone is the sorrow and anger on his face because now he knows he doesn't have to marry someone else. That memory knots in my chest with a surge of desperation at how close we came to having both our lives ruined. But that's the past now, and I refuse to hold onto that fear any longer.

"Is this your secret getaway place?" I ask, stepping inside, taking in the little clear globes filled with lights hanging on the walls, making the place appear magical.

Ahren steps toward me and takes my hand, drawing me into his arms instantly. The magnetic attraction is instant between us as I push myself onto my toes, our mouths meeting. His kiss is hungry and fast like we haven't seen each other in months. I return the passion, grasping onto his shoulders, pressing my breasts against him.

Strong hands wrap around my back, sliding down, cupping my ass.

I can't breathe with the desire of how much I crave him. Mouths join together, our bodies pressed tight, it hits me how much I would have lost if he married someone else. To never feel his touch, his lips, his body would have killed me.

"I never thought I'd be with you again," he breathes against me. His lips fell to my neck, where his licks and small bites sent shivers through me.

His words coat me, as does his fear of losing me. TThe breath I draw in hitches, mirroring my own dread. I knew this already but to hear it from him means everything to me.

I cup the sides of his face, whispering, "We're never going to be apart again." Then I kiss him with an addictive fever, and he responds with a raw, primal growl, his fingers digging into my lower back. I give a soft moan as he takes handfuls of my dress, bunching it up around my waist. He breaks from me suddenly and kneels in front of me.

My chest heaves with breath as I wait to see what he'll do.

Fingers curl over the top of my underwear and tug it down my legs. I step out of them as his hand, feather-soft, touches me across the apex of my thighs, over the small mound of hair, while holding the material of my dress up. Ahren just stares at my pussy like he's taking in what he hasn't seen for a while, and kisses me there so tenderly, my heart flutters. Though he moans with a hunger that drives me crazy with lust.

He's on his feet in seconds, a hand behind my head, and he pulls me in. We kiss again, his other hand tugging the fabric down my shoulder so harshly, my whole body shakes. But I don't care, not when I'm starved for this fae.

My breasts pop free, and he lowers his head, sucking on my pebbled nipple.

"Please make it hurt," I ask.

His gaze drifts up at me and smiles, then he gnaws on my nipple harder, while his other hand finds the heat between my legs again. Fingers slide between my soaking lips, parting them, and he pushes two fingers into me unceremoniously.

I throw my head back, groaning, giving myself to this fae. He traces his mouth over my collarbones, my throat, and he kisses me, bruising my lips.

Everything about him calls to me.

My hands thread through his hair, holding onto to him as he releases his fingers from within me.

"Fuck me, Ahren," I purr.

His smile is wicked, and I clench my thighs, my clit pulsing just at the way he stares like he's about to devour me. He unbuckles his belt and pants, dropping them so quick, he's naked from the waist down in seconds. His thick cock is hard and moist on the tip. God, he is so big and I want him inside me.

"Come here, beautiful. I haven't been able to stop thinking about your delicious little pussy, and how much I'm going to fuck you."

My ovaries more than approve, and my whole body clenches at the sexiness of his words. I grab hold of his black top to drag him to me but he lifts me off my feet by my waist. I coil my legs around his hips, deftly lifting the skirt of my dress between us with one hand.

"Take me," I demand. "Show me how much you've missed me."

"When I'm finished with you, the whole kingdom will be breathless."

A shiver runs over me, and I shudder from his words alone.

He adjusts me slightly, until the tip of his cock kisses my entrance. I'm wide and spread for him.

"I make you a promise," he says, slowly pushing into me. "That every time we fuck, you will scream and beg for more."

Writhing against him, I tilt my pelvis to take him easier, to fit him. "Then show me already," I challenge him.

Grasping my hips, he sinks into deep in one long thrust. I scream out, partly from the best kind of pain, and mostly from surprise at how fast he takes into me. I grip his strong, round shoulders as he fills me completely. There's no pause as he fucks me standing up, his mouth on my neck

I moan and squeeze him inside me, the friction between us an inferno. He walks us over to the lounge, where he lays me onto my back effortlessly, one of his hands on the cushion, the other on my back. He remains embedded inside me the whole time. He is so strong.

Shifting slightly to accommodate him from this new angle, I lean forward and we kiss.

Our bodies are one, moving in rhythm, our breaths in a dance. My nipples prick the quicker he pummels into me. He's relentless, showing no sign of slowing, and I'm drowning in his passion, our sex scent, in the way he claims me. His lips caress my neck, while his hips drive into me, over and over.

"Oh yes, fuck me harder," I plead.

I'm floating on the clouds, loving every damn second of the way he makes love to me. I surrender completely to him.

We fuck, and I adore those sounds he makes… they are pure bliss. I am so turned on, his thrusts are incredible.

My entire body trembles, and a powerful shudder of euphoria coarse through my entire body so quick it surprises me. The orgasm comes suddenly, tearing through me. I scream out with pleasure, my back arching, as he keeps crashing into me, over and over, shaking the chaise lounge.

A thunderous growl rumbles out of his throat. His grip on my hips tightens, and after a final plunge, he pauses inside me, pulsing. He roars, and I fucking love him. I can't stop staring at this gorgeous man lost in his own lust, buried deep inside me. And he's mine. All mine.

We're both breathing heavy, sweat beading across his brow.

He collapses on top of me. "You are fucking beautiful, and I love everything about you." We stay embraced, locked together for I don't know how long, but I don't want to move. This is where I want to be always.

His breaths brush over my neck as he finally pulls back from me. He slides out of me and goes to collect his clothes, dressing himself. Then with my underwear in his hand, he cleans me up, then tucks them into his pocket. I can't help but adore the way he cares for me.

I shuffle to sit upright, drawing my knees to my chest as I cover them with my dress. He flops down near me, our sides pressing together like neither of us can bear to be apart from each other for more than a few seconds.

"My intention was to talk to you first," he says, half laughing. "But I have no control around you."

Cradling in against his chest, I embrace the contentment that fills me. "That was perfect. I missed you so much."

We don't talk right away. He holds me, and I let

myself start to believe that what I have is real. Then I decide I need to tell him things he doesn't know. I clear my throat and say, "I wanted to tell you about my father earlier. But I didn't want to come across like I'm taking your throne. I never wanted it, Ahren. In truth, all I cared about was not losing you."

With the way he looks at me, I see the hurt in his eyes like my words have taken him aback.

"Guendolyn, I would never think anything less of you if you'd told me the truth. And I should have been truthful about my arranged marriage the moment I found out. I kept hoping someone else would break the news to you. I didn't want to lose you, so I put off the inevitable." He wraps an arm around me, drawing me closer. I melt against this big, powerful fae who wants me as much as I do him. "We both tried to protect each other and only made things worse," he admits.

I rest my head against his shoulder, breathing in his masculine scent of fresh soap, pine, and our sex. "Pretty much. But we ended up together in the end. That's all I care about."

"I want to hear everything," he coos, while kissing the top of my brow. "Tell me how you first met your mother, how you found out who you were. I feel like I missed out on so much to make sense of it all."

For the first time in too long, I feel calm. There's no secret to conceal, no worry about what tomorrow will bring, no one hating me. Well, not that I'm aware of.

So, I take a long breath and explain the events from recent days from Jasion kidnapping me, to visiting my mother, the ruby shards in my hand, and even to Ramond helping us.

His hold tenses, and I sense him stiffening at hearing me. I expect him to bombard me with questions, but he doesn't. When I glance up at him, his expression is of someone distraught.

"You know the rest as you were there in the great hall yesterday," I say, but he doesn't meet my gaze. "Did I say something wrong?"

He still doesn't speak, and the struggle on his face intensifies, slicing through me that something is seriously not right here.

"Talk to me," I prod.

"You were in danger and hurt, and I did nothing," he murmurs, almost as if he's speaking to himself. His voice darkens.

The piercing ache in his voice rips me apart

because the point of reflection is to understand and learn, then move on, right?

"Ahren."

"No, I was meant to protect you. I did nothing to stop you from being hurt." His jaw clenches, and he stiffens against me like he's shutting off.

Except we've come too far, overcome so much, to let this get in our way.

I turn to face him.

"I'm alright." He takes my hands and kisses the palms of both. "But I should have been there for you."

"You're here now. That's what matters. We both did what we thought was right at the time." I kiss him, stealing the hurt from him, replacing it with my love.

He doesn't break away, but when I break our kiss, he leans his head against my chest. I hold him like that for a long while. We all deal with pain in our own ways, and if he needs me to just hold him, then I'll do that.

I lose track of how long we stay bound together, and when he finally comes up, he just cups my face and kisses me. Tenderly, filled with love and affection. This isn't about lust or desire, but the true feelings he holds for me inside. That's why he hurts.

"I know I can't undo the past, but I will show you how much you mean to me every single day for the rest of our lives together."

I laugh as happy tears prick my eyes and I hug him. "That means the world to me."

Three Days Later

I stare into Luther's gaze as he stands next to me grinning madly, dressed impeccably in deep blue pants and a doublet jacket, with a gold coat that hangs from his broad shoulders like a cape. The color matches the gold buttons running down the front of his jacket, bringing out the color of his amber eyes. Each time I look at him, my knees wobble... but let's be real here. All three princes have the same effect on me.

Deimos stands next to him who winks my way, rousing giddiness inside me, while on my other side is Ahren. Tall and proud, dressed similarly to his brothers except in a deep red and silvery suit.

His smile is spectacular, the corners of his eyes crinkling, his strong jawline drawing my attention. I am so in love with my princes that it still overwhelms me.

Ahren leans toward me and whispers in my ear, "I'm going to ravage you tonight."

A shiver of delight zips down my spine and curls in the pit of my stomach, recalling our time in the garden hut, and arousing the beast that is my libido. She's completely out of control around them.

So I lean in and repay the favor, whispering, "I'm not wearing any underwear today."

The change in his expression is instant, lust gleaming in his eyes.

Normally I would laugh at him, but this may not be the most appropriate of places. I glance out to the thousands of fae spread throughout the Ash Court grounds, made up of both Seelie and Unseelie, here to celebrate our marriage and our acceptance of the throne. After this, a spectacular revelry is planned. Mother, who sits in the front row next to the princes' mother, arranged this for us.

Looking at the attendees, my stomach flip-flops with nerves. I don't think I will ever get used to this kind of attention.

The late afternoon sun is setting, coloring the sky in an array of bejeweled reds and oranges and pinks. Hundreds of fairies sit in the branches of the surrounding trees, watching and taking part in our gathering.

"Your Highnesses," Michae announces and bows before us. He's dressed in a crisp new guard's uniform, his shoulders lined with the golden stripes of the captain. His new role, which he quickly accepted.

Behind him, several guards drag forward the old king of Ash Court and his mother, hands tied behind their backs, a blue aura around them. Courtesy of Ramond to ensure their magic is blocked.

My mother had them captured and imprisoned the day she arrived at Shadow Court, keeping them locked safely away until we could make a decision.

"Drop to your knees," a guard bellows as he kicks in the back of the king's legs. He falls, and his mother follows suit on her own.

My mother gets up from her seat. She looks

incredible, dressed in a pale green dress that flows loosely to the floor, the hems and sleeves made of fabric as thin as a spider's web, her hair pulled off her face by a tiara made of flowers.

She looks at me. "My Future Queen, I realize we are doing this a bit backward, but I don't want anything to interrupt your marriage and coronation. The decision is yours on what we should do with these two."

The old king studies me with contempt, with hatred, while his mother might very well be poisoning me with her glare. I've been pondering this moment for the past few days as we prepared for the event, knowing this was coming.

I step forward on the large dais, the diamonds on my billowing princess dress glinting from the numerous lights strung around the grounds and the fiery torches peppering the land.

"I don't know either of you very well," I say, "but my whole life, up to this point, has been a lie because of you. I grew up without my real family, thinking that I was going crazy. You took away everything from me. And as much as I'd like to think you've learned your lesson and would never harm me again, that's not the case, is it?"

Their deadpan stares answer my question. Not that I'm surprised.

"You are a curse on our realm" the old woman spits. "You will rip it apart and wreak havoc with your tainted existence."

I square my shoulders, lifting my chin, and despite the anger curling around me, I refuse to give her what she wants. To see me lower myself to their level.

"That's where you're wrong. I will unite the fae like they once were, like the fairy queen would have wanted. There will be no more war, no more death and bloodshed, but a realm where fae aren't afraid of their own kind. Your militant leadership ends now." I lift my gaze to Michae. "Take them to the dungeon!"

"No," the old king pleads. "We ruled this kingdom for years; please, show us mercy. There is no reason to condemn us to death."

I feel no pity for him, because he had years to make right what he did to me. I don't trust him in the least. "Take them," I repeat, louder this time. "You tried to kill me, and for that you will have your power stripped and sent to Earth to spend the rest of your days. Get them out of here."

"You're a fucking whore who will destroy this

realm!" The old king gets to his feet, writhing against the guards' grip, bellowing curses.

While his mother cries about injustice, then turns on me, "I should have killed you as a baby instantly."

Her words make me sick to my stomach. I turn my back to them and return to my princes, who smile with admiration.

"You were perfect," Deimos says.

Then why am I trembling with nerves of the confrontation in front of a crowd? I take slow breaths to calm myself.

It isn't long before an elderly fae in a long white coat buttoned from his thighs to his neck approaches us. White hair drapes halfway down his back, and he smiles so gently when he meets my gaze.

A soft tune permeates the air, the fairies serenading us as they move from the trees to hover amongst the guests. The sight and sound of their beautiful wings beating, blending with their humming tune, brings a sense of love to my heart.

The guests join in, and I can't stop smiling, because I know what's coming.

My whole life I've struggled. I fought to just feel

normal. To fit in. To stop being an outcast. But this feels right—I'm exactly where I should be.

The elderly fae stretches a ribbon of lace between his two hands. "Place your wrists on this band," he instructs.

The four of us crowd together and follow his instructions, after which the officiant proceeds to tie our hands together with a nice little bow.

He then begins to speak in a language I don't understand—an ancient fae language, I'm guessing —but I get the gist. He is marrying us, uniting us as one family as he holds our bound wrists in his palms.

My chest beams with warmth, and that earlier giddiness spreads through me, because this is real. There are no more tricks or secrets.

The girl who was lost, who had nothing, is marrying three princes. Tears prick my eyes, and I blink them away, because I won't cry. My princes all look at me, smiling, and I wish more than anything it was just us four and not so many onlookers. I'm trapped, my emotions bubbling within me to the point of exploding while trying to act as casual about this as possible. But it's a losing battle.

Looking from Deimos, to Luther, and then to

Ahren, I know I made the right decision to fight for us.

Once the fae pauses, he lifts our hands and kisses each one in blessing, then undoes the ribbon from around our hands. "You may now exchange rings."

A flash of panic races up my back as I realize I didn't get rings for my princes. With everything else going on, it hadn't crossed my mind.

All three of them drop to one knee in front of me, loving me with their eyes and smiles.

Ahren takes my hand first and presents me with a gold ring embedded with a pink, star-shaped diamond. I gasp. "It's beautiful." And then I start giggling—never in my life did I expect such dreams to come true for me. It sparkles like a disco ball as he pushes it onto my fourth finger. I wiggle my fingers at how perfectly it fits perfectly on my middle finger.

"May it always brighten your path so you never forget you are loved," Ahren says.

I melt on the inside, and I lean in to embrace him, except Deimos takes my hand and I quickly straighten back up.

He slides a ring on my index finger, a white gold band with the reddest ruby in the shape of a teardrop. "A reminder of the beauty that lies inside your heart and that it will never steer you wrong."

I grin crazily at him, chewing on my lower lip. I just want to throw myself at him and kiss him all over.

Next Luther takes my hand, and his half-smirk says it all. We've come such a long way, him and I. From when he entered my mind with his smartass flirting, to bringing me to this realm and fighting for our life together.

He takes my hand and rubs his thumb over his grandmother's ring I wear on my wedding finger. "For my little wolf. Never stop fighting for what you believe. It's one of the many reasons I fell in love with you."

And with that, I completely lose control of my emotions. Tears fall and drench my cheeks; I can't stop crying with happiness.

My princes stand and embrace me, all of us as one. "You don't even know how much this means to me," I manage to say between sniffling and wiping my eyes.

"Yes we do," Ahren says. "I love you so much that it killed me to almost lose you."

"I love everything about you," Deimos says.

"And I loved you from the beginning," Luther adds.

I huddle against them, tears streaming down my cheeks—then I start laughing like a crazy person. "These are all happy tears, you know that."

They chuckle with me, and Ahren wipes my cheeks with his thumbs. "Are you ready to continue, beautiful?"

"Yes. Let's do this."

My mother waits a few steps away, her eyes also glistening, and she hands me a small box. I find three rings inside, all a dark gold with different patterns carved into the bands. I collect them into my palm as I mouth *thank you* to her.

Then I turn to my princes and push my ring on their fingers, one at a time, each beaming with joy.

The crowd cheers—fairies included—as the officiant declares our marriage. It all feels surreal.

The elderly fae has left the dais, and now the head council members, one from each court, step forward.

Behind them are four young girls, carrying a silky pillow with a crown on it.

My heart beats faster, anticipation curling in my chest. Ahren removes his cape from his shoulders and lays it on the floor before me. He then takes my hand, murmuring, "We must all be on our knees."

They kneel down, then I take Ahren's hand and do the same, all of us in a line, and I am the first the councilmen come to.

I shake with excitement, wishing I had my phone so I could take photos of everything and not forget a single memory.

One of the councilmen approaches with a small crystal bowl filled with liquid. He dips two fingers into the liquid, then runs them across my brow and down my cheeks. He speaks fae words again, which I assume are a blessing and the anointment of my new role. A young girl steps forward carrying the most spectacular tall crown, pebbled with rubies and white gems to match my wedding dress. The other councilman, so councils from both courts are involved, lays it on my head. It's a lot heavier than I anticipated, but it sits perfectly.

I can't stop beaming, convinced I'm about to cry again, while I watch the princes receive their crowns, gold and dotted with colored gems. I actually pinch my arm to make sure this is real. I've always heard people say that when they got married, the day flew by at lightning speed. That is how this feels.

"Please embrace our new Queen and Kings of Ash and Shadow Courts," the council members announce in unison.

At that, the masses break out into a cheer, the fairies singing louder, fluttering around us and filling the sky with a rainbow of colors. As we climb to our feet, the fairies' song explodes into its crescendo, and everyone claps louder. The band chimes in, and then an array of staff in white suits come out of the castle nearby, carrying silver platters of drinks and food.

I'm utterly dumbfounded that I am now Queen. It's going to take a bit of getting used to.

"What happens now?" I ask Ahren.

"We have fun and kiss you a lot." He takes my hand and leads me down the steps, and I keep reminding myself—this is my wedding reception. It's time for me to party and celebrate—because I won. I got what I wanted in the end…my three fae.

"Where are we going?" I ask Luther as he drags me down one hallway, then another. "Do you even know this place? What about the guests outside?"

"Of course he does," Deimos answers from beside me. Ahren is at my back, all four of us heading through the Ash Court castle. This is our new home... well, one of two, really, and I still don't know where we will end up living. Part of me is toying with the idea of expanding one of the courts to bring everyone to live in one location, united. Wherever we end up, we'll plant grand trees for fairies to live in, if they choose.

But that comes later. Right now I need to know what my kings have in store for me.

After hours of celebration, they snuck me out, insisting they had a surprise.

We rush quicker, the three of them smiling wickedly while I laugh. Nothing in my life has ever felt so secure. So perfect.

Coming to a halt in front of a grand arched door, Deimos turns toward me. "We spoke with your mother and discovered something you'll find interesting. King Tibout purchased the ruby for his throne because he knew his daughter had a direct lineage to the fairy queen, as did the ruby that might assist with your powers, even though he told nobody. He had intended to give you the ruby if he ever had a chance to meet you. I'm not saying this to upset you, gorgeous, but to let you know he loved you."

His story touches me, and all I can think about was the last time I saw my father. Our conversation over wine. I wish so much that I would have known then he was my father so I could have told him it was me.

Luther's hand is at my back, rubbing small circles.

Deimos swings open the door, and before me lays a beautiful, grand room that whisks me away into another world.

Pearlescent walls dripping with green vines covered in small white flowers. Rows and rows of white benches, as though we've stepped into a gothic church. A fresco of fairies and flowers on the lofty ceiling. There are freaking real trees along the back wall, filled with green leaves and flowers, the ceiling there made of glass to let in natural light.

In front of the trees are four thrones, all black with golden patterns to match my husbands' rings. The high backs are engraved, except one is different. A ruby stone is embedded into the crest.

"Is that—"

"Yes," Ahren answers. "Your little friend Hiss

had another ruby the fairies were guarding, and she is gifting it to you."

I want to run outside and hug her. My cheeks are now officially hurting from smiling so much. It's still hard coming to terms with all of this, but it doesn't stop me from twirling on the spot. "You did this for us?"

"Well, magic was involved," Luther tells me and leads me forward by the hand.

Deimos shuts the door behind us, and once I take my seat, it's Ahren who stands in front of me. The other two are to the side—it's like they have their own ceremony planned.

"What's going on?" I ask, finding my throne rather comfortable as I recline and look out into the room. The seat is wide and can easily seat two people, so naturally I picture myself snuggling in it with one of my men.

My crown, along with the princes'—no, kings'—have been put safely away for now, but a girl could get used to wearing it and sitting up here.

"This room is brand new, as are the thrones. And we figured this would be the perfect time to break them in," Ahren announces. The way he stares at me is different from the serious expression I'm used to. Today he is playful and flirtatious, and I completely love seeing him happy for a change.

He falls to his knees before me, and I straighten in my seat. Except, he takes my ankles and tugs slightly so I'm slouching again.

"Whoa." I grip the armrests to avoid tumbling off.

"I remember you made me a promise," he teases, his hand slithering under my gown and crawling up my legs to my knees.

My heartbeat intensifies as heat coils deep in my gut. "Yeah, and what is that?" My breath catches in my throat as his hands pry open my legs as much as the seat allows, which is quite wide, apparently. Is this why they build them so large?

"I haven't been able to think about anything else but you not wearing any underwear." Ahren's touch slides between my thighs, his fingers grazing the heat, the inferno, the melted puddle of what they all do to me.

"Fuck! I need you," he growls and pushes the fabric up as he tucks his head under.

Before I can respond, he grips my hips and drags my ass to balance on the edge of my seat, placing me in prime position.

My heart beats hysterically as arousal intensifies with fury through me.

"What if someone comes in and... Ahh." I throw my head back, clasping the arms of my throne as Ahren's mouth clasps over my pussy.

Unrelentingly, his tongue flicks as he devours me like an animal.

I'm crying out, groaning, while Deimos and Luther close in, both of them bunching the fabric of my wedding dress around my waist.

"We need to see this," Deimos insists.

Luther is already unbuckling his pants, staring down at Ahren eating me out, my legs spread wide.

I pat the fabric down so I can see my kings get off as much as I am. Ahren pushes two fingers into me, tugging on my clit with his mouth. Fire streaks through me, the warm heartbeat between my thighs growing in intensity.

The euphoria rushing over me comes fast, and I'm not sure how much longer I'll last.

"I want to fuck you bending over the throne," Deimos coos.

Now, if being a queen means having your pussy licked and claimed by the three most insanely handsome fae in the world, well... I'm fucking intend to be the best Queen this realm has ever seen.

I look back and love the feeling after the ceremony... After everything I've been through, I finally found my home.

ABOUT MILA YOUNG

Best-selling author, Mila Young tackles everything with the zeal and bravado of the fairytale heroes she grew up reading about. She slays monsters, real and imaginary, like there's no tomorrow. By day she rocks a keyboard as a marketing extraordinaire. At night she battles with her mighty pen-sword, creating fairytale retellings, and sexy ever after tales. In her spare time, she loves pretending she's a mighty warrior, walks on the beach with her dogs, cuddling up with her cats, and devouring every fantasy tale she can get her pinkies on.

Ready to read more and more from Mila Young?
Subscribe to her newsletter
www.subscribepage.com/milayoung

For more information...
milayoungarc@gmail.com